SECRETS AND SOULMATES

RACHEL HANNA

PROLOGUE

She stood in front of the house, her insides trembling. This was it. This was the moment she'd been waiting for. Everything about her life was about to change, and she was going to be with the man she loved more than anything.

They would finally be together after over a year of texting and occasionally talking on the phone. No more staring at his picture every night on her computer screen before she fell asleep, wishing and hoping he could be there holding her as she drifted off to sleep. No more wondering what it would be like to hold his hand or have him give her a great big bear hug after a long, hard day.

Everyone had made fun of her. Everyone had questioned her. But they were all wrong; they had to be. Never had she gambled so much in her life by taking everything she owned across the country to a tiny little beach town for one reason only – love.

She felt paralyzed in place, like her feet were stuck in two large blocks of cement instead of placed on the top of a non-sticky sidewalk. She couldn't seem to get herself to move forward, to finally knock on the door and end all the suspense.

He had no idea she was coming. No idea that they were about to be together. He'd be so happy, so relieved that she was finally there in front of him. He'd said it so many times before, that he couldn't wait to meet her, to see her, to touch her.

Yes, she was finally going to have the last laugh with her friends and family. They'd see they were all wrong, and that her romantic notions for this man who lived thousands of miles away were so much more than anyone could've imagined.

They'd have this amazing love story, something they could tell their kids and their grandkids. The kind of love that people write books about. It was just on the other side of that door, she thought, as she reached her hand toward the big brass knocker shaped like a seashell.

And it was just like every other amazing love story. Except for one thing - she'd never met him in real life. She had never seen him even on Skype or video chat. And right now, she prayed to God that he wasn't just some figment of her imagination.

CHAPTER ONE

Molly James had two loves in her life, animals and a guy named Blake. The problem was, she only got to spend time with one of them in real life.

At twenty-two years old, she wasn't really where she wanted to be in her life. School had always been hard for her, much to her parents' dismay. Growing up in a family where everyone else seemed to be on the level of genius, Molly had struggled. A lot.

High school had been the hardest, by far, mainly because she barely made it from one grade to the next. But even that would've been cool if she hung around with that kind of a crowd, but she also happened to look the part of a nerd during her formative years.

Petite with auburn hair and green eyes, she looked more like one of the boys than one of the girls back then. Before she had learned how to do her makeup properly, the freckles on her face were what she was most known for, aside from her inability to read the way her peers did.

Of course, she finally learned that she had dyslexia in her sophomore year of high school but it was too little too late. Trying to learn new ways of studying with only a couple of years left of school proved to be almost impossible. And when her SATs came around, the embarrassing number she saw on her scoresheet almost sent her into a total depression.

Her parents were hard on her and not nearly as accepting of her dyslexia as others. They wanted her to be something she wasn't, just like her extremely smart brother, Liam.

Oh yes, Liam was the apple of their eye. He'd almost gotten a perfect score on his SATs, and was now working in Silicon Valley at a tech firm and dating a girl who could only be described as prettier than Barbie. At two years older than Molly, Liam set the standard for what her parents expected.

But she was not what they expected. She was nothing like the rest of her family, often leading her

how to answer the current question that was on the table. Addison must've picked up on her unease.

"I'm so sorry, Molly. I don't mean to pry."

"No, it's just that I don't really know how to explain why I'm here. You're going to think it sounds kind of silly, just like my family and friends."

"Well that sounds intriguing, but I won't pry anymore. If you want someone to talk to, just know that I'm here. I've lived in January Cove for my entire life, so if I can help you with anything around town please let me know. In the meantime, let's get you set up in a room."

She scooped up her baby and took Molly upstairs. She showed her the second room on the left, which was a beautiful space with hardwood floors and pale pink walls. The thick moldings and tall windows truly made her feel transported back to the 1800s when the house was built.

After going over the cost to live there, it became really clear to Molly that she needed to find at least a part-time job quickly. She could survive a couple of weeks, but anything longer than that was going to require a regular income.

"How's the job market here in January Cove?"

"Well, it's a small town so there's not a whole lot to choose from but I do know that my soon to be sister-in-law is in need of a cashier at her coffee shop."

"Oh, that sounds right up my alley. I have quite a fondness for caffeine," Molly said with a smile.

"Then you're going to want to taste the Guatemalan blend I've got brewing right now. Why don't you come downstairs and have a cup with me? I can fill you in on all of the details about January Cove, answer any questions you have..."

Molly nodded. That sounded like a fabulous idea to her.

SHE HAD ONLY BEEN in town for about 24 hours, but Molly was falling in love with January Cove. It was a quaint town with nice people who always greeted her when she passed them on the street. It wasn't the hustle and bustle of the big city that she had grown used to, living so close to Seattle, and she was kind of enjoying the slower pace.

But next on her agenda had to be the one reason that she came there in the first place. She had to go see Blake, and her nerves were getting to her as she held his address tightly in her hand walking through the square.

It was only about five minutes from the bed and breakfast, and she'd been so nervous up until now that there was no way she could imagine going to see him. That morning, she had even gotten up and meditated which was something she didn't normally do. It didn't really help. Her heart was still thumping and pounding, and she'd never had as much sweat running down her back in her life.

She turned the corner to see the small cottage where Blake lived. It was a pale yellow color with green shutters, and it looked like something out of a beach magazine. He literally lived steps from the sand, and she couldn't wait to spend the evening sitting on the beach, drinking wine and staring into each other's eyes.

She slowly made her way up the walkway to the front door, and found herself looking at the seashell door knocker for too long. Her knees were knocking together, and she was almost positive that people walking by would be able to hear them.

"Okay, you've got this. On the other side of that door is the love of your life," she whispered to herself. Then she took a big breath and pulled the door knocker back, rapping it against the strike plate twice. And then she waited.

She could hear someone walking towards the

door, so she stepped back a couple of feet and smiled. He was going to be so surprised to see her standing there. He would probably grab her immediately in a firm embrace and then give her their first passionate kiss. Or maybe he'd tear up when he finally saw her face to face, happy and relieved they could finally be together.

Instead of seeing her handsome Blake, an older man opened the door. He was short and pudgy and bald, and he looked just as confused as she did.

"Before you ask, I'm not interested in buying any magazines or wrapping paper..." he started. "And I already know God." There was a smell emanating from the house that seemed to be a mixture of sweat and Italian food, and it was assaulting her nose in a way that made her gag reflex start to activate. She stepped back another foot.

"No, sir, I'm not selling anything." She was rather confused because Blake had never told her that anyone else lived there with him. His father lived in Hong Kong and ran a business there, but he didn't have a relationship with him anymore. Maybe this was a roommate?

"Ma'am, can I help you with something?" he asked.

"Oh, sorry. I'm looking for Blake," she said with a

smile. This guy wasn't the most pleasant person in the world, but right now he was her only link to Blake so she felt a fondness for him just the same.

"Blake who?" Her stomach lurched.

"Blake Wells. He lives here."

"No ma'am, he doesn't live here and I've never heard of him."

"I'm confused. Blake and I talk all the time. And this is the address he gave me." Truth be told, she never sent anything to his address, but he'd given it to her once simply by sending her a postcard. It had the little return address sticker on it, but they spent most of their time talking on the phone or texting so she never had any reason to send him anything in the mail. That's when it dawned on her. Maybe he had moved recently and just hadn't told her for some reason. Why would he do that?

"Well, I don't know why anyone would do that. I've lived here for fifteen years all by myself, and I've never heard of anyone named Blake."

All of a sudden, the world started spinning and the next thing she knew everything was black. When she opened her eyes again, her head was resting on some pine straw in the bushes beside the front door and the older man was hovering over her.

"Are you okay, ma'am?" the man said, shaking her

shoulders with his hands. God, had he eaten an entire onion for breakfast?

"I'm fine. What happened?" she asked as she slowly sat up with his assistance. He was huffing and puffing, red faced and sweaty. The last thing she needed to round out this terrible day was for him to have a heart attack and land on top of her. She'd probably just will herself to have a heart attack as well at that point.

"Well, I assume you got overwhelmed when I told you I don't know Blake. Should I call the ambulance?"

She shook her head. "No, I'm fine. I must've just gotten a little overheated." She got up to her feet, and although she still felt a little bit woozy – probably because she hadn't eaten that morning yet – she didn't feel she had a need for medical attention. Right now, she just wanted to go back to her room and curl up in the fetal position.

"Thank you for your time," she said as she started to walk down the sidewalk.

"I hope you find who you're looking for!" the man called to her. She hoped so too.

MOLLY HOBBLED BACK to the bed and breakfast, still a little bit dizzy headed and more than a little bit confused. Her heart was breaking, knowing that there was a possibility that Blake didn't live in January Cove anymore and maybe wasn't even real. She kept trying to figure out the reason why he didn't live in that house and never had. Why would he send her a card with a return address if he never lived there?

All of these things were running through her mind as she walked up the sidewalk towards the bed and breakfast. She wanted to go inside, shut the door and sit in the dark for a few hours. She ambled up the steps, opened the front door and heard a loud "ouch" and then a crash.

And then there was a man laying at her feet.

"Are you okay?" she said as she looked down at the man that seemed to come out of nowhere. He was laying flat down on the floor of the porch, arms and legs sprawled with a paintbrush in his hand. Where had he come from?

"Are you blind or something?" he asked as he turned over and sat up, tossing his paintbrush aside. He came up to his feet, put his hand on his hip and stared at her. "Hello?" he said, waving a hand in front of her face.

He was a jerk. A cocky, arrogant jerk. But to be fair, she had just thrown him on his face somehow, although she still didn't know how she did it.

"What happened? I didn't see you…"

"Well, obviously. You were walking up the stairs like you were some kind of ghost. You didn't even look my way. I can't believe you couldn't see me down here beside the door painting this trim. Never expected you to knock me on my face with a screen door."

"I'm really sorry. Obviously, my mind was somewhere else. It certainly wasn't intentional." She didn't really know what else to say, but right now she was on the verge of bursting into tears and it wasn't in her plans to do that in front of a perfect stranger. Plus, he was the most handsome person she'd ever seen, but also seemed to be a big jackass so she wasn't in the mood to deal with that right now.

"Maybe you need to get your eyes examined," he said before turning around and picking up his paintbrush.

Molly knew she should've walked away, left the guy alone, but she just couldn't do it.

"You know, has it occurred to you that maybe I've had a really bad day and just wasn't paying attention. Or are you this much of a jackass to everybody you meet?" She stood there in her little red sun dress with her arms crossed and her hip jutted out.

He looked at her with a crooked smile, which was extremely sexy but irritating. "I'm this much of a jackass." And with that, he turned and went back to painting the trim without a word.

"Well, I can believe that!" she shrieked before bursting into tears and running into the bed and breakfast. Yes, it was an embarrassing way to handle it, but her emotions overtook her.

A few minutes later, there was a knock at her door. If that was the jerky guy, she was going to pull her hair out by the roots.

"I'm busy right now," she said through stifled tears.

"Molly, it's Addison. Are you sure you don't want to talk?"

Molly opened the door slowly, her eyes puffy and red. Addison said nothing but pulled her into a hug. After crying on Addison's shoulder for a few minutes, Molly finally pulled back and laughed.

"You must think I'm a crazy person."

"No, I get the feeling you are a person who's in love with someone and something has gone terribly wrong?" Molly nodded and sat down on the edge of the bed.

"I came here because I wanted to surprise the guy I've been talking to online for over year. I know it sounds silly, but he proposed to me recently. I lost my job, so I decided to take a chance on romance. I packed up everything I own and drove all the way here from Washington state."

"Wow! What an amazing story. So what's wrong? Did he reject you?"

"No. It's just that I'm not sure he exists."

"I don't understand," Addison said as she sat down next to her on the bed.

"I went to the house where he supposedly lives and a man answered the door. That man has lived there, alone, for fifteen years."

"Oh no. Maybe he just moved…" Addison tried to make her feel better.

"I don't think so. I think I got played."

"Well, I know everyone in town. I grew up here and have basically lived here my whole life, so I can definitely tell you if I've heard his name."

"Blake Wells is his name," Molly said, the last remnant of hope attached to her words.

Addison took a deep breath. "No, honey, I've never heard that name." Molly's dreams were shattered in that instant. It was obvious that somebody was playing a trick on her, but she had no idea who would do such a thing.

Molly started crying again, devastated at the turn of events. She'd picked up her entire life and gone all the way across the country, and there was no way that she could go home empty-handed. Her parents would throw this in her face for the rest of her life, and Olivia would be right. She'd be a total idiot, trusting anyone who told her anything. How could she have been so stupid?

"I guess I need to pack my things," Molly said as she stood up. Addison stood up and faced her.

"You're welcome to stay here as long as you want. Maybe you didn't come all the way here for Blake."

"What do you mean?"

"Maybe the love of your life is actually here but his name isn't Blake. Maybe fate brought you here for a different reason and you should stick around long enough to see what it is."

Addison was obviously a romantic. Either that or she was just trying to make Molly feel better.

She thought about it. Maybe she was right. There was nothing back home for her except memories of being picked on and parents who didn't think she was smart enough to make good decisions.

She decided to stay in January Cove, at least temporarily, until she could figure out what she wanted to do with her life. One thing was for sure – she wasn't going to let her parents or Olivia know that Blake probably didn't exist. So if nothing else, January Cove provided a great hiding place until she could figure out her plan B.

CHAPTER FOUR

A ustin stood at the job site, which was right next to the ferry dock, and looked out over the land. He wasn't sure what Mr. Ballard was thinking when he bought this property. It was small, long and narrow, and although it was beautiful overlooking the water, he couldn't figure out exactly how they were going to build a restaurant and have enough parking space.

If there was one thing that January Cove was short on, it was land. And they certainly weren't making any more of it. He'd called Mr. Ballard that morning, and the older man had promised that he was sending along the survey soon to show exactly how he wanted it laid out.

And he wanted Austin to stay in January Cove for

at least the next several months to make sure that the property was built to his specifications. This was an unusual deal because Mr. Ballard wasn't just developing the land. He planned to have someone on his staff actually run the restaurant because he was using it as a retirement investment.

All Austin knew was that he needed to do his best work to impress Mr. Ballard so that maybe he could move up within the company and one day help to run it with his best friend, Eddie. That was his long-term goal anyway, but he had no idea if Mr. Ballard had the same thing in mind.

"So when does building begin?" someone said from behind him. It was Clay, the owner of the bed and breakfast where he was staying. Clay seemed like a nice guy, a man's man with a kind demeanor.

"Oh, good morning. We're hoping to start in another couple of weeks. Just waiting on the surveys and permits to be finalized. What are you doing here so early?" Austin asked as he shook Clay's hand.

"I run the ferry. Not a lot of activity going on at this time of the year, but I'm always here in case someone needs to run to the island or over to Savannah."

"The island?"

"Yeah, there's a little uninhabited island that a lot

of people like to go to, pick up seashells, picnic. You know the drill."

The truth was, Austin hadn't done a lot of looking around yet. He was pretty hyper focused on his goal – do a good job for Ballard and make a name for himself in the business. Money wasn't even his focus. Lord knows, he'd grown up without any of it himself. He just wanted to be his own man and chart his own course.

"I didn't know you ran the ferry. Seems like that would be a very seasonal job," Austin said.

"It is, but it's just a little side business and something I do because I enjoy it. It definitely wouldn't pay the bills," Clay said with a smile. "So how are you enjoying January Cove?"

"I actually haven't had a lot of time to look around yet. Been pretty focused on the plans for this place," Austin said, pointing at the land in front of him.

"Well, if you need a little tour, be sure to let me know. I've been here my whole life."

"I can't imagine growing up someplace like this," Austin said. "I grew up in the city." The way he said it made it sound like he grew up in some magical place, but the part of the city that he'd grown up in wasn't exactly what he'd refer to as magical.

she'd had experience working in retail, so it would be a smooth transition.

Addison gave her the details on finding the place, which was called Jolt and run by a lady named Rebecca. She walked down the sidewalk in the quaint little town, the sound of the ocean just off in the distance. Even though she'd grown up near the ocean herself, this place was different. Cozy. Full of families. Full of promise.

The square was like something out of the 1950s, complete with a barber shop and antique store. January Cove felt preserved in time, and the people were a part of that too. Everyone she passed along the way spoke, smiled or waved at her. She knew everybody had their own set of problems, but you'd never know it here because most people were all smiles and Southern charm.

She walked through the door of Jolt, a little bell dinging to signal her arrival. Rebecca was behind the counter, or at least she assumed that's who it was by the description that Addison gave her of a woman with fiery red hair.

"Welcome to Jolt!" she called with a smile.

"Thank you. I'm Molly. Addison told me to come," she said, hoping that Addison had told Rebecca who she was.

"Oh yes. I'm so glad you're here. I had a teenage girl working here for a couple of weeks, but she sort of flaked out. My son was helping me out behind the counter, but he's really busy in high school and playing football, so I need some help."

"Well, I'm glad because I need a job," Molly said, feeling a little awkward. Rebecca seemed nice, but she definitely didn't want to make a fool of herself and ruin her chances.

"So when can you start? I need someone who can work the morning shift until lunchtime. It's five days a week and maybe the occasional Saturday."

"You mean I have a job?"

"If you want it," Rebecca said with a laugh. "The pay is ten dollars an hour. I know it's not much, but I think it will cover your living expenses at the bed and breakfast at least."

"That works fine for me. I'm looking forward to starting!" Molly said, and she really was. Surprisingly, she was looking forward to this new chapter in her life and having something to call her own without any interference from her family.

Molly had been thinking about what she could do on the side that would bring in some extra money, and dog walking seemed to be a good option. Addison explained that they had a lot of tourists coming into the area at different times of the year, and hiring a dog walker would be of interest to those people as well as the locals.

But for now, she'd focus on the coffee shop and worry about starting a business later.

After chatting with Rebecca for a few more minutes, they decided that she would start the next morning. Molly was looking forward to it, but what she wasn't looking forward to was explaining what had happened with Blake to her family and friends. She had no idea what she was going to do about that, and she still wasn't completely convinced that he didn't exist... somewhere.

IF THERE WAS one thing that Molly couldn't figure out, it was whether or not Blake actually existed. At first, she was certain that he didn't when she saw the man standing at the door of the house in January Cove. But now, she wasn't so sure.

He had been texting her every day, like clockwork – just like he always did. Because she wasn't sure who she was dealing with, she hadn't mentioned that she was right there in town. She wanted to see if she could get any additional information.

But now she was more confused than ever. She had asked him for an address to send him a care package, something she hadn't done in many months. But he told her he was busy traveling with his family because his grandmother was sick.

The only problem was, she thought his grandmother had died. She could've sworn he already told her that, but some of their older text messages had already been erased so she couldn't prove it.

On the off chance that he was real, she just went along with things until she could prove it one way or another. Maybe the love of her life was really out there, going to see his sick grandmother in South Carolina just like he said he was.

But that still didn't explain why the old address that she had written down wasn't where he lived. In fact, he had never lived there at all. She was having a hard time getting around that in her mind.

Maybe she had written the address down wrong. Since the old text message was gone, she had no way to verify it. And she had left the old postage slip back home, opting instead to write it down on a piece of paper before she left town.

She certainly couldn't call her parents and ask

them to look through one of her boxes to find the slip. They would know then that something was up for sure.

So she continued on, acting normally, hoping against hope that he was real.

One day soon, she would tell him where she was and that he needed to come find her. She just had to work up her courage first. And every fiber of her being hoped that he would arrive on a white horse, whisk her into his arms and show the world he was most definitely real.

As she stood behind the counter on her second day of working at Jolt, she was easing into the slower paced lifestyle of January Cove. And, she was starting to like it.

Every person she'd met had been nice to her, with the exception of the jerky guy who was staying at the same place she was. She had managed to stay away from him since knocking him over on the porch, and she planned to keep it that way.

At least she thought she could keep it that way until she heard the door ding. There he was, walking through the door looking at her as if she was beneath him in some way. Even his face was cocky.

"Welcome to Jolt," she said with about as much enthusiasm as someone in a coma. She didn't crack a smile and tried not to make further eye contact. Rebecca was gone to spend the day with her boyfriend, but she probably wouldn't be happy with the way Molly was greeting her customer.

"Well, that was a lackluster greeting," cocky guy said. A hint of a smile started to appear on his face, but it was more sarcastic than friendly.

"What can I get you?" she said, still trying to avoid eye contact.

"What do you recommend?" he asked. What was with this guy? Why couldn't he just order a coffee like a normal human being and be on his way?

"I don't know... Coffee, maybe?" she said, giving him the sarcasm right back. It was 7 o'clock in the morning and she was in no mood for regular conversations much less long talks with the most arrogant guy she'd ever met.

"Yeah, I think coffee would be a good idea. I have a very hard time dealing with people until I get some caffeine."

"Well, you must've been decaffeinated when I met you the other day then," she heard herself saying without thinking. Why was she continuing to engage this guy in conversation?

"Wow, you get right to the point. Yes, I actually was decaffeinated that day."

He stood there, with all the confidence of a high-powered executive, but she could tell that wasn't the type of work he probably did. He was wearing a nice pair of jeans, a golf shirt and he certainly wasn't carrying a briefcase. In fact, the town didn't seem like a place that would play host to corporate bigwigs anyway.

But she had to admit to herself, he was good-looking. It was just a shame that he was so arrogant. No normal woman was ever going to want to spend time with a guy like that.

He wasn't wearing a wedding ring which made sense because she couldn't see anyone wanting to be married to him either. She wasn't into New Age stuff, but she could almost see an invisible aura around him like a wall keeping the world out.

"Well, then can I recommend a double shot of espresso for you this morning?" she said, forcing a smile. Amazingly, he smiled back and this time it didn't look as sarcastic.

"I think I better stick with regular coffee. I'd hate to be zipping around town without a car. I'm not sure this little town is ready for me on two shots of espresso," he said, pulling his wallet out of his back pocket.

"So you're new to town also?"

"I thought that was kind of obvious since I'm staying at the bed and breakfast."

"I wasn't sure since you seemed to just be doing some work there."

"No, I offered to do a few things for free. Clay and Addison seem to be nice people."

"They do. I'm glad I got to meet them."

"So you just moved here too?" he asked, and suddenly she got uncomfortable. They weren't going to be friends, and she had no desire to tell him her life story.

"Just visiting for a while," she said as she slid the cup of coffee across the counter and took his money. She opened the cash register, gave him his change and smiled. "Thanks for stopping by." Without another word, she turned and started wiping down the counters. A few moments later, she heard the door ding and saw him out of her peripheral vision walking down the sidewalk.

Disaster averted.

TESSA REEVES STOOD in front of the long mirror in the corner of her bedroom, her wedding dress flowing across the floor behind her. It was the perfect dress for her. She felt like a fairy princess and couldn't wait to get married to her prince.

Since moving into her soon-to-be mother-in-law's old house, she and Aaron Parker had started to build a life together. With her wedding coming up in just a few days, she was more excited than ever to finally become his wife.

Still, it made her sad to think that her mother wouldn't be at her wedding. After losing her mother when she was only ten years old, and then her father dying in prison when she was nineteen, Tessa had been alone in the world for a long time. Even when she was married to her abusive husband, she was still really alone.

But being a part of the Parker family had changed her life. Her son, Tyler, had just turned four years old and thought of Aaron as his father. She couldn't wait to have more children, this time with a man who truly loved her and her son.

"Knock knock!" she heard a voice say from the foyer downstairs. It was Jenna, her soon-to-be sister-in-law. Jenna was married to Aaron's brother, Kyle.

"Come on up!" Tessa called.

"You're wearing it again?" Jenna said with a laugh as she walked into the room. Tessa seemed to be wearing her wedding dress more than she was wearing her regular clothes these days. But somehow she had managed to keep it hidden from Aaron, not wanting to jinx herself before the wedding.

"I certainly paid enough money for it, so I figure I should wear it at least once a day," Tessa joked. She enjoyed the company of all of the women in the Parker family, but felt particularly close to Jenna. They had experienced similar issues with men in the past with Jenna's ex-husband being mentally abusive, although Tessa had also experienced pretty severe physical abuse.

"That's true, but I'm thinking you might be over-dressed for our lunch date today."

"Oh my goodness! I'm sorry. I totally forgot." Tessa started rushing around the room, trying to unzip herself with no luck. Jenna reached over and unzipped the dress while Tessa scurried into the bathroom to change clothes.

"And I thought I was the one losing my mind," Jenna said with a laugh. "Pregnancy brain is already starting to get to me. This morning, I almost forgot to take Kaitlyn to school. I thought it was Saturday."

"I remember what that was like," Tessa said.

"I'd be willing to bet that you'll have another baby

pretty soon." Jenna was already lobbying for Tessa to get pregnant as soon as she got married so they could be pregnant together for a while.

"At least wait for me to get married first!" Tessa said laughing.

"All right, but you have to hurry up if you want to catch up with me. This baby is already causing me to gain weight, and I'm not that far along yet!" Jenna said. And it was true. She was already starting to show a little bit, of course on her tiny frame it wasn't hard to show any extra weight.

Tessa zipped her wedding dress into the bag and hid it in the back of the closet. She knew that Aaron wouldn't be seeking her wedding dress out for any reason because he was pretty traditional too, but she wasn't taking any chances. In fact, she would be staying away from black cats, walking under ladders and broken mirrors until her perfect wedding was behind her.

CHAPTER FIVE

Molly sat on her bed, her feet aching after a long day of work. Standing up all day and waiting on customers had proven to be a lot more exhausting than she would've anticipated.

But so far, she liked her job. Still, her plan was to get back to working with animals as soon as humanly possible. Truth be told, she really enjoyed dealing with dogs more than she did people.

And every day like clockwork, the cocky guy kept coming into the coffee house. He said it was his regular place to go, and wasn't she lucky that she had to be the one to wait on him every day.

She also had some other regular customers like Rebecca's boyfriend, Jackson. He seemed like a nice guy, but he was always in and out quickly because he had a lot of work to do. Rebecca was rarely there these days as she was helping to run some of Jackson's online businesses, but she came by once or twice a day to check on the place and make sure that Molly was okay.

Another regular customer was Brad Parker, one of the siblings that apparently ran the town. He was overseeing the development of a new shopping complex in January Cove, although his girlfriend was helping to run the Lamont Theater which had been renovated into a tourist attraction.

The one good thing about working at the coffee shop meant that she got to hear all of the gossip from the town and learn everybody's back story. She kind of liked that.

But right now, all she wanted was a nice hot bath and a quiet evening in her room. Dinner would be served downstairs in another hour, but she usually didn't go down there for that. Most of the time, she grabbed something in town but tonight she was pretty tired and figured she'd take them up on the offer of having a home cooked meal.

She walked into the bathroom and started the water, but before she could get into the tub her phone rang. It was her mother, and she thought for a moment about not answering it but knew that would only worry her and make her come looking for her. Her mom didn't have very much patience.

"Hello?"

"Molly! Where have you been? Olivia said she's been texting you for days but not getting any response. We were starting to get worried."

"I'm sorry. I found a job here, and I've been really busy working."

"A job? I thought you were just going for a bit of a visit with... What's his name... Brent?"

Molly sighed. "Blake." It amazed her that she could be talking about a guy for a year now and her mom still couldn't remember his name.

"Okay, Blake. But I didn't know you were getting a job."

Her mom was like a bulldog. Once she got a hold of something, she did let go.

"I've decided to stay here for a while, so I needed to get a job."

"What kind of job?"

"At a coffee shop."

Her mom made a grunting noise on the other end of the phone. "You're working at a coffee shop? Oh, Molly..." She made it sound like Molly was living in a homeless shelter.

"Mother, it's fine. It's a great little town and I like my job. Once I get settled, I'll find a veterinary clinic."

"Get settled? Just how long are you planning to stay there?"

"I don't know. I'm a grown woman. This is the choice I've made for right now."

"You know, you don't sound nearly as happy as I thought you would. This Blake character... What's his deal? Is he not what you thought?"

Her stomach clenched up. Now was decision time. She had to figure out what to say to keep her mother and everyone else off her back while maintaining her dignity.

"He's wonderful. He's everything I thought he was, and we're getting to know each other on a much deeper level. So I decided to stay around and see where it goes."

In any other person's life, their mother probably would've left them alone but not in Molly's life. Not Molly's mother.

"I think you should come home. I'm sure we can find another position at another veterinary office, but I don't like the thought of you being alone in that town across the country with some stranger."

"Mom, I'm happy. You've got to let go."

She could dream that her mom might actually hear her words and let go, but she knew it would never happen. Either way, she was at least able to get off the phone for right now and procrastinate on what to do next. For now, she was going to forget the phone call, lose herself in a hot bath and then enjoy a home-cooked meal with nice people.

Or so she thought.

AFTER A NICE LONG BATH, Molly ventured downstairs, following the smell of what she could only assume was pot roast. From what she could tell, Addison was a great homemaker. Her baby was starting to crawl around quite a bit more lately, so Molly had to step over a baby gate at the bottom of the stairs.

The bed and breakfast was small and not fully occupied during this time of year, so when she saw Clay and Addison and their baby sitting at the table, she assumed it would just be the four of them. And then cocky guy appeared from around the corner, dressed nicely like he was going out to a four-star restaurant.

Molly looked down at her spandex workout

pants and oversized T-shirt and felt immediately out of place.

Cocky guy looked at her with a smirk of a smile as if he knew she felt like a fish out of water and pulled out her chair. Shocked, she stepped to the right and pulled out a different chair and sat down. She thought she heard him chuckle under his breath, and then looked at Addison and Clay who seemed to be oblivious to what was happening as they dealt with their baby bucking in the plastic highchair at the end of the table.

"I'm sorry we're a little bit out of sorts tonight. I think Anna Grace has an ear infection and she is not in the best of moods," Addison said. She looked tired with big bags under her eyes.

"No problem. You know, when dogs at my veterinary clinic had ear infections, we sometimes put hydrogen peroxide in their ears. Have you tried that?"

"I haven't. But I'll ask the pediatrician about that…" she said as she tried to calm the little girl. It wasn't working, and she started crying and turning red. Addison picked her up and started rocking her while she stood beside Clay.

"Maybe we should take her in?" Clay asked.

"I think so too," Addison said. She looked apologetically at Molly and Austin. "I'm so sorry, but do you guys mind eating without us?"

"No, we totally understand," Molly said, as if she spoke for the both of them.

"Go. We've got this handled," Austin said with a smile.

Clay and Addison went straight out the front door, and Molly could hear their car pulling out of the driveway moments later.

She sat there for a few seconds as Austin moved across the table from her and smiled.

"What?" she asked as she started to put mashed potatoes on her plate.

"I guess it's just the two of us."

"Yep," she said, still not making eye contact.

"You don't like me, do you?" he asked as he grabbed a fork full of pot roast and slapped it onto his plate. He surely didn't have the table manners to go with those clothes.

"I don't even know you."

"I'm Austin York, twenty-six year old sexy man from Atlanta. And you are?" he asked, reaching out across the table to shake her hand with another sarcastic smile plastered on his face.

"Not interested," she said, finishing his sentence.

Austin laughed and used his hand to pick up the pitcher of sweet tea and pour himself a glass.

"You're a spitfire. And I know your name is Molly."

"Excuse me? How do you know that? Have you been asking Addison or Clay about me?" She was livid that this perfect stranger was digging up any kind of information about her.

"Um, no. Conceited much? Jeez."

"Then how do you know my name?"

"Hey, coffee girl, you wear a name tag at Jolt."

Ugh. She felt like a complete idiot. There was nothing she could do but laugh, so that's exactly what she did. Amazingly, Austin laughed too and it looked good on him. He should do that more often, she thought.

They ate in silence for a few minutes, the only sound a barking dog off in the distance, as the Georgia sky turned all shades of pink and orange. She'd never seen such beautiful sunsets as the ones in January Cove.

"So, what are you doing in this tiny little town?" he asked, basically repeating his question from the coffee house.

"I told you I'm just visiting for a while," she said, taking a bite of the roast. It was amazing and made her miss the big Sunday lunches her grandmother made when she was a kid.

"Visiting who?" he pressed.

"Why do you want to know?"

"Because I'd rather hear you talk than listen to you chew."

"Do I chew loud?"

"Let's not find out." His smile was nice when it wasn't mocking her. "So who did you come here to visit?"

She really didn't want to talk about it, but he wasn't letting up. And now she had an entire dinner to eat plus clean up since Addison and Clay weren't home. There was no chance of escape.

"Fine. I came here to find a guy I'm engaged to." It even sounded stupid now that she heard it coming from her mouth.

"Wait. What?"

"Nevermind."

"No, come on. I'm intrigued now. You came to find a guy you're engaged to? What does that mean? You haven't found him yet?"

"No."

"Is this a riddle?" he asked with a laugh.

"I wish."

"Spill it, Molly. What's going on?" For once, he

sounded a little concerned, almost like a friend. Maybe she could trust her secret to this one cocky guy who didn't know anyone back in her old life anyway. What would it hurt?

"Met a guy a year ago online. Fell in love. Got engaged. Came here to surprise him."

"Okay. Weird, but where is he?"

"It's not weird. He loves me, and I love him."

"And you've just Skyped and stuff without ever meeting?"

"We haven't Skyped…" she muttered under her breath, hoping he wouldn't hear her.

"Wait. Did you say you haven't Skyped? Or seen him on video at all?" Now he was interested and leaning over the table, his elbow resting in a small blob of mashed potatoes on the table.

"Maybe get a napkin," she said pointing.

"Don't change the subject. This is fascinating."

"Why is it fascinating?"

"How do you fall in love and get engaged without meeting someone in person?"

"Because what's inside matters more." Now she was just trying to convince herself.

"You at least saw pictures, right?"

"Of course."

"And you thought he was hot?"

"What are you getting at?" She was started to get irked.

"If what's inside is all that matters, then why did you care what he looked like?" He sat back in his chair and crossed his arms, obviously delighted with himself.

"Shut up, okay? I've had a seriously long week already." She stood up and raked off what was left on her plate and put it in the dishwasher. Austin scooped another spoonful of roast into his mouth before doing the same.

Molly started putting the food away, searching through cabinets to find plastic storage containers. Of course, they had to be too high for her to reach. She stood there, on her tippy toes, trying her best to get them until Austin walked up behind her - too close for comfort - and grabbed three of them.

They worked like a team, him carrying the food from the table to the counter, her putting it into the containers. She left them on the counter to cool before putting them in the refrigerator.

"So was he everything you hoped he would be?" he finally asked as she was wiping down the table. He stood against the breakfast bar with his arms crossed, and she truly wanted to smack the smile off his unbelievably handsome face.

"I don't know. I haven't seen him yet."

"What? You've been here for a few days and you haven't made the attempt to see him?"

"I didn't say that exactly..." she said, but she was interrupted by her phone ringing. Perfect distraction. She pulled it from her pocket without looking and said hello.

"Finally! Have you been avoiding my calls?" Olivia shrieked on other end.

"Of course not." Total lie.

"Well, how's it going? Your mom said you have a new job?"

"Yep, at a coffee shop," Molly said as she continued wiping the table. Austin stared at her with an intensity that made her get chills.

"Okay... Well, what about Blake? Was he surprised to see you?" Olivia prodded.

"He was. Totally," she said, trying not to say too much.

"And how is he?"

"Good..."

"Molly, you sound weird. Is everything okay?"

"Yeah. I'm just really tired. Can we talk about this later? I promise I'll call you tomorrow."

Molly hung up the phone and went back to trying to avoid eye contact with Austin. He seemed really serious all of the sudden, like he could read her mind.

"He wasn't real, was he?" he finally asked. She stopped and looked up at him.

"You're kind of nosy. You realize that, right?"

"Yes, but answer my question."

"It might just be a big misunderstanding, but the guy who lives at the address I had for him has lived there for a long time and doesn't know Blake. Has never heard of him. But Blake told me he's traveling right now…"

"Molly, you've been catfished."

She knew the term, and hearing it made her cringe. She wasn't a stupid woman, and there was no way she'd fallen for a scheme. No way.

"No, I haven't."

"Do you have his picture?"

"Yes, of course. It's on my laptop upstairs."

"Come on," he said as he walked up the stairs with her not far behind.

"Um, you can't go into my room," she said as he pushed the door open and walked inside. What on Earth was wrong with this guy? He clearly didn't understand personal boundaries.

Austin walked to her computer, which was sitting on her bed and opened it.

"What's your password?" he asked. Molly snatched the computer from his hands.

"Do you have no sense of privacy and space? Get out of here."

Austin looked at her, serious again. "Don't you want to know the truth?"

Did she? She wasn't sure anymore. Holding out hope that the love of her life was real was the only thing holding her together. Being all alone, thousands of miles from the only home she'd ever known was more than enough to bear.

But she needed to know.

"Yes. I want to know."

"Then let me help you. We can figure this out, at least whether he's real or not." He held his hand out, motioning for the computer. Molly sat down on the bed across from him and typed in her password. She pulled up the pictures of Blake and turned the computer around. Austin smiled.

"He's... preppy?"

"No, he's not!" she said, unsure of why that would be a bad thing anyway. "He just has style."

"Alrighty..." Austin said under his breath. She scooted behind him a bit, keeping a careful distance, as she watched him click around. He opened a page, dragged her image onto it and suddenly results started appearing below it.

"What does that mean?" she asked, unsure of what she was seeing. She had never been very good with computers, even though she should've been just because of her age. She could work her phone and tablet pretty well, but computers always reminded her of school and she avoided them as much as possible.

He turned a bit and looked at her. "I hate to tell you this."

"What?"

"This guy isn't Blake." He actually did look pained when he told her, and if she wasn't mistaken, he looked a little angry too. She wasn't sure at who, but it was definitely there under the surface.

"And how could you possibly know that for sure?"

"See these results? Those are all pointing to a modeling site. When you click here, you can see this guy's name is Jared Allred. Not Blake."

She sat back on her knees and stared straight ahead, willing herself not to break down in front of Austin. She took in a deep, albeit ragged, breath and bit her bottom lip.

"I don't understand..." she said softly. "Why would anyone do this..."

Austin closed the computer and pushed it away. He turned around and looked at her. "I'm sorry, Molly. Sometimes people are just mean. Sometimes, people just suck."

He definitely had a way of cutting to the chase, and it made her wonder how he had become so jaded in his own life.

"Yeah, it's why I like working with dogs," she said without thinking. He smiled.

"I'm sorry. I really am, but better to know that it was all a fake so you can move on," he said as he stood up and took a couple of steps toward the door. "Now, I saw banana pudding in the fridge. Wanna share it?"

"Are you kidding me?" she asked.

"What?" he said, a look of confusion on his face as he leaned against the doorframe.

"I just lost the love of my life and you want me to eat pudding?" She stood up and crossed her arms. "Don't you have a heart?"

Austin furrowed his eyebrows and then laughed. Molly didn't see anything that was funny. "Don't you think you're being a bit dramatic? You didn't lose the love of your life. You were catfished, and it sucks, but let's be real here. How gullible do you have to be to believe a person you've never met? And you even agreed to marry this person who you haven't seen, hugged, kissed…or, ya know…"

"Don't… finish that sentence," she growled through gritted teeth. "I guess we're different people, Austin York. I believe in true love and the fairy tale, and apparently you believe in… what? Nothing?"

He went stone faced for a moment and jutted his chin forward. Definitely a defensive posture. And for a moment, she was scared. She didn't know this guy at all really, and he was now in her bedroom. And she had potentially offended him. And they were alone in a house. And she was across the country from everyone she knew. Throw in a little horror music, and she was in every 80's scary movie.

"I believe in myself," he said before he turned and walked out without another word. She thought he was going for pudding, but instead she heard his door shut down the hall. He didn't slam it, but instead shut it quietly which made her wonder what Austin York was running from in his own life.

CHAPTER SIX

Austin sat on his bed and ran his fingers through his dark brown hair. There was no reason to let this woman shake him. She meant nothing to him. She was a nobody, just some woman he was trying to help.

He didn't care.

The only problem was - he did.

This had never happened to him before. Women were a dime a dozen, but developing feelings for them just didn't happen. He didn't allow it. There was no time for a relationship at this point in his life.

Trust was for sissies, and he wasn't a sissy. He did the hard work. And he wasn't dragging some emotion-filled broad along with him.

So why was she getting to him so bad right now?

He reached for his cell phone and opened Facebook, trying to get his mind off of her.

She was adorable. Short, petite, girl next door. She was sassy, sarcastic and far too trusting.

To think that someone had taken such advantage of her... it bothered him. He couldn't help it. Maybe it just made him a decent person. It meant nothing.

He scrolled through his newsfeed looking for a distraction. Oh look, another cute puppy video. And a cat video. And a wedding dance video.

He tossed his phone across the bed and laid back against his pillow. He had really wanted that banana pudding. Was it too late to sneak downstairs and have some?

Addison and Clay had come home a while ago, and they were in bed now. Maybe he could just have one bowl. Gosh, he loved banana pudding. He never got that kind of stuff as a kid, and the couple of times he'd had it were when Eddie's grandmother had made it for him.

He threw on a pair of sweatpants and a t-shirt and slipped downstairs, being careful to make as little noise as possible. He didn't want to wake the baby, and he didn't want to get caught with his hand in the cookie jar, so to speak.

The only light on downstairs was a small lamp on

the breakfast bar. He crept into the kitchen, being careful to avoid any squeaky floorboards along the way. He opened the refrigerator to reveal his prize - a huge clear glass bowl of banana pudding.

Only one scoop seemed to be missing, so he assumed Clay had already dipped into the snack himself after coming home from taking his baby girl to the doctor.

He filled a bowl with the dessert and decided to go outside to enjoy it. It was October and cool, but certainly not so cold that he couldn't spend a few minutes sitting in the garden behind the house.

It was a beautiful full moon, and Clay had just installed some solar lights in a circle around the garden area. Being careful to close the door quietly behind him, Austin was really thankful that the B&B didn't have an alarm system.

He sat down on one of the concrete benches and looked up at the bright moon. It made him feel small, but not in the way that his rough childhood had made him feel small. Looking at the moon, he always felt like he was a tiny speck in the huge universe around him and the opportunities to live the life he wanted were endless.

Just being in January Cove was a big deal to him. Being at the beach was something he could've only dreamed of as a kid. There were never any family vacations or long walks down the beach picking up seashells with his mother. In fact, the first time he'd seen the ocean in person was when he turned twenty-two and scraped up enough money cutting lawns to take a bus to the Gulf Coast.

He still struggled with things from his childhood. Trust issues. Being defensive. Fake arrogance. He knew that he was really still that scared kid under all the bravado, but he felt safer that way. Even at twenty-six, that scared kid controlled what he said and did every day of his life.

He took his first big bite of banana pudding, closed his eyes and savored it like it was his last meal on death row.

"Mmmmm," he heard himself say out loud.

"Enjoying that, are you?"

Startled, he squinted his eyes and realized that Molly had been sitting on the bench across from him the whole time. She had her own bowl piled high with pudding. Thus the mystery of the missing scoop was solved.

She looked freaking adorable and sad at the same time. Wearing a fluffy pink bathrobe - God knew what she was wearing underneath, if anything - and fluffy slippers, she sat there with her puffy red eyes and massive mound of pudding.

"You scared the crap out of me!" he whispered loudly. She stayed where she was.

"Sorry. I thought I'd get some alone time out here." She took a bite and stared at her bowl.

The quiet of the night was broken by the sound of crickets and the low roar of the ocean in the distance. Originally, he'd thought the quiet life would be hard to adjust to, especially since he'd spent all of his years listening to honking horns, police sirens and the occasional gunfire.

But he was starting to love January Cove. There was just something about it that made him feel at home.

"Listen, Molly…"

"Please, Austin, I can't take much more tonight. I've cried so much that I think I might have warped the floors of my room, so can you just… not talk?"

Why was this so painful to watch? She was a stranger, he kept telling himself. But he had this nagging feeling that she needed a hug. He wasn't about to attempt that, but maybe she'd let him sit next to her quietly.

He slowly walked toward her and sat down next to her. She didn't move or look at him, and he made sure to leave a good foot of space between them. She smelled like lavender.

"You were right," he said, surprising himself. He wasn't one to admit he was ever wrong.

"About what?" she asked softly, still staring straight ahead.

"I don't believe in anything."

"What about God?" she asked.

"I don't know what I believe about God. I wasn't exactly raised with any kind of faith."

"But you're a man now, so can't you choose what you believe?"

"Yeah, I guess you're right."

"So, do you believe there's a God?" she pressed.

"Why did you start with the hardest question first?" he asked with a laugh before sitting his now empty bowl on the other side of him.

"I know how you like to cut to the chase," she said, cracking a little smile as she cut her eyes at him.

"Good point. Okay, yes, I believe there's a God. I've seen too many miracles in my life."

"Really? I'd love to see some miracles."

"So what about you? Do you believe in God?"

"Of course."

"You say that like it's a foregone conclusion."

"For me it is. I've always believed. I have to. I

want to believe in miracles." Her voice was crackly from crying, and he felt bad suddenly. Maybe she'd been crying about how he'd acted. But then he remembered that she was probably crying over the loss of what she believed was her one true love.

"I'm sorry I made fun of your situation."

"I accept your apology," she said quietly. She was silent for a moment and then finally spoke again. "I guess I was naive. I just wanted to be wanted, for once."

Her honesty made his heart hurt. What had this girl gone through?

"Somebody will want you, Molly. You're young and beautiful." Ugh. He had to shut up now.

She turned and looked at him with a slight smile. "See? That was very nice. You have the ability to be nice, Austin."

He laughed. "Doubtful. I think I'm just high on banana pudding."

They sat silently for another couple of minutes. "I want to know who did this to me. I need to know who caused me to take leave of my senses and even move across the country. I don't even know where to start…"

"I do." What was he doing now? It was like his

mouth had been overtaken by aliens. He didn't have time for this right now!

"You do?"

"Yeah. I think we start with the address you have."

"But I already went there. The guy had never heard of Blake."

"Because Blake doesn't exist. But maybe he's rented his house before or something. We can start there."

"We?"

"Look, you're alone in January Cove. I'm alone in January Cove. Two stranded tourists. I'll help you as long as you promise me two things."

She smiled. "What?"

"Number one, you don't poison my coffee."

"Hmmm…. Plans for tomorrow are scratched now. Okay, fine. What's number two?"

"Number two is that you," he said, leaning closer to her face so that their noses were almost touching, "don't take so much of the banana pudding next time."

And even though she laughed, it was a nervous laugh, and that told him just what he needed to know. Molly James was attracted to him, and he had to be careful. This was no time to make the biggest mistake of his life.

MOLLY SHUT the door to her room and leaned against it. Oh no. Austin was flirting with her. She just knew it. And he wasn't her type. He wasn't the one for her. At. All.

She'd thought he was about to kiss her, and the sad part was she might've let him.

Maybe she needed medication because her brain wasn't wired properly. She'd followed a cyber ghost across the country to marry him - a total stranger. She'd left her family and friends and pretty much all career prospects to become a cashier at a coffee house. And now, she was tempted to kiss another stranger who seemed to have his own set of emotional problems and a slight addiction to banana pudding.

Oh, this wasn't good.

AUSTIN STOOD at the job site watching his workers clear the land for Ballard's new restaurant, but his mind was elsewhere. He couldn't stop thinking about Molly and finding the jerk who had made her cry like that.

Last night had been scary and amazing at the same time. Scary because he was feeling things he'd never felt, and he wanted those feelings to just go away. But he also felt amazing at the same time because he could help her. He knew he could.

But what would helping her accomplish? Make her fall for him next? Is that what he wanted?

"Dude, are you listening to me?" one of his workers, Jerry, said from in front of him. Austin was standing there, clipboard in hand, staring blankly at a mound of dirt.

"Huh? Oh, sorry, man… I was thinking about something."

"A woman, huh?"

"Of course not!" Austin said as he turned toward the temporary trailer he had sitting at the site.

"A man?" Jerry prodded as he followed.

Austin turned and glared at him. "No."

The two men went into the trailer which had some much needed air conditioning. Although it was October, occasional warm days were the norm in January Cove at this time of the year.

"What's up?" Austin asked as he sat behind his

little desk and took an apple from his lunch bag. He bit into it and sat back.

"We've got a problem with the backhoe. I'm going to need to call the repair guy, but that's going to set us back at least two days even if he's on time."

"Damn it!" Austin shouted. The last thing he needed were setbacks. This would bring the whole job to a standstill, and how was that going to look to Mr. Ballard?

"Man, there's nothing I can do. I just wanted you to be prepared. That backhoe isn't even that old, so I have no idea how long it will take to fix it."

This wasn't good news at all. The whole site would be silent for at least two days, and that wasn't going to do anything for his reputation with Ballard.

"Stay on top of it, Jerry," he said, leaning across the desk. "Don't make me ask for an update."

Jerry nodded and walked out of the trailer quietly. The men who worked with Austin knew him to be young, but very tough. No excuses, no passing the buck.

There was a faint tap at the door. "What now?" he yelled. The door opened, but it wasn't Jerry standing there. It was Molly.

She was wearing her Jolt apron, and her eyes were still a little puffy from the night before.

"Hey. You got a minute?" she asked softly.

"Of course. Come on in," he said, standing up. "Everything okay?" Were his hands sweating? Yep, his hands were sweating.

"Yeah. Listen, I didn't see you at Jolt this morning…"

"I got here early. Brought my own coffee," he said, holding up his insulated cup as if he needed evidence.

"Hey, I promised I wouldn't poison you," she said with a slight smile. "And I only crossed the fingers on one hand."

"Very funny. Actually, I just needed to get here before Jolt opened. And who's minding the store right now?"

"Oh, Rebecca stopped by for a bit and gave me a break. I think she knows something is up with me today." She sat down in one of the chairs across from his desk, so he sat back down too. Apparently, she was staying awhile and he didn't have a problem with that at all.

"Glad you got a break." He had no idea what to say to her. All of it felt awkward.

"I just came by to say thank you for helping me last night."

"I made you cry, Molly."

"No, the whole situation made me cry," she said, which was good to know but also meant he caused part of it. "I feel like such a fool. You were right. How gullible I've been."

She looked incredibly defeated, and he knew there was more to it than just this guy.

"Better to take a chance once in a while than to never find someone special." What was he saying?

She looked up at him and smiled, as if his words had been a surprise to her. "I don't get you. One minute you're so gruff and straight to the point, and the next minute you're sweet and kind. Who are you, Austin?"

He smiled. "I have no idea."

"I'll accept that. I also came to ask you another question."

"No, I won't marry you." He immediately regretted it after he'd said it. Way too soon, idiot. But she laughed. Loudly. And he wasn't sure what to think about that.

"Thanks for the laugh. Anyway..." she continued and his heart was stuck in his throat. "You mentioned helping me find Blake... or whoever the heck this person is. Were you serious?"

"Totally serious. I love a good mystery."

"Good, because I want to find this person and

pound their ass into the pavement," she said with a completely straight face.

"Dang, girl! That's something I never thought I'd hear come from your mouth." He was almost a little proud.

"You don't really know me, Austin," she said with a sly smile. "I can be, what was it you called me, a 'spit-fire', when I want to be. I'm over the crying phase, and now it's on to the payback phase. Care to be my partner?" She reached her hand across the desk, and he hesitated for a moment. He had the distinct impression that this handshake was going to change his life.

So he shook her hand.

TESSA AND JENNA stood in the tiny church, each with a measuring tape in hand.

"I don't see how we can fit all of these groomsmen up here. These are big guys, Jenna."

"Well, I can starve Kyle for a few days, but I don't think that helps with Brad and Jackson." Tessa laughed. It was all she could do given that her wedding was just two days away and it felt like nothing was done.

"Oh crap! I forgot to go approve the flowers. What time does the florist close for lunch? Lunch! I forgot to eat lunch!"

Jenna closed the space between them and put her hands on Tessa's shoulders. "Deep breaths," she said with a smile. "Everything's going to be fine. It's going to be the most beautiful day of your life."

Tessa took a deep breath and smiled. "You're right. I know I'm getting so totally insane over this, Jen, but I want everything to be perfect. I finally found my perfect soulmate, and I don't want anything to mess that up." She sank down onto the wooden pew and sighed.

Jenna sat down beside her. "You know, when I was little, my family used to attend this church."

"You did? It's adorable."

"I remember my aunt Margie got married here when I was about eight years old, and I was the flower girl. I was terrified. I swear my knees were knocking."

Tessa giggled. "I can't imagine you being scared of much."

"Well, I was. I thought I'd trip because my mom made me wear these little heels, and I had never worn heels before."

"But everything went perfectly and you worried for nothing…"

"Nope. I tripped."

"What kind of story is that?" Tessa asked with a laugh. "This isn't making me feel better!"

"Not only did I trip, but I threw up because I was so anxious. Thankfully, these wood floors can't be stained because it was pretty bad since I'd had red jello right before the wedding. Unfortunately, Aunt Margie's dress didn't fair so well. It had one of those long, Princess Diana style trains and it was white. Snow white. When I was finished, it looked like Aunt Margie had been shot at her own wedding."

Tessa couldn't help but laugh at Jenna's story, although it wasn't doing anything for her confidence. "And why are you telling me this terrible story?"

"My Aunt Margie and Uncle Paul have been married all these years, and they are some of the happiest people I know. Those little hiccups at the wedding are fun stories that we told at the holidays, but they didn't change anything about their love and the life they'd go on to have together. They have four kids now and a beautiful love story, Tessa. No matter what, you and Aaron will have the same. It's just one day on the calendar."

Tessa hugged her friend and soon-to-be sister-in-law tightly. She knew she was right. Being with Aaron had already been her greatest blessing in life second only to her son, Tyler, and marrying him would just be the icing on the cake

CHAPTER SEVEN

"Good morning!" Molly called to a customer as they walked through the door of Jolt. She didn't recognize this woman, but she was almost regal looking with her stylish blonde hair and air of confidence.

"Good morning to you too. You must be new around here," the woman said with a smile. Molly hadn't seen her before and wondered how she would know that. "I'm Adele Parker."

"Nice to meet you. Molly James," she said, reaching out her hand and shaking Adele's. "I haven't seen you around here, but then I've only been here for a week or so."

"My daughter in law… well, I consider her to be my daughter in law… Rebecca owns this place."

Then it hit her. Adele Parker! Jackson's mother. Addison's mother. Rebecca spoke fondly of her often. She was like the matriarch of January Cove, but Rebecca said she'd been traveling with her new love for a few weeks now.

"Ah, you must be in town for the wedding. I've heard Rebecca talking about it a lot lately."

"Yes, my son, Aaron, is marrying Tessa. Wonderful couple. We're very excited for the big day tomorrow!" Adele said, gushing with pride.

"Well, congratulations on adding to your family. Can I get you something?"

"I'd love a latte, light foam please."

Molly went to work behind the counter as Adele took off her jacket and sat down at one of the bistro tables nearby.

"So, is Rebecca around?"

"Actually, I think she's with Tessa this morning. Some final wedding preparations from what I gathered," Molly said as she frothed the milk.

"Yes, there's a lot going on, for sure. It's so good to be back home for a few days."

"Heading on the road again soon?"

"Yes. My husband, Harrison, and I, are hitting the road yet again! Planning to head out west for a few weeks before coming back here for the holidays."

"Thanksgiving?"

"No, we won't make it back in time for that, but my kids will survive without me," she said with a smile. "Sometimes, it's just the end of an era, you know?"

"Yes, I know that all too well," Molly said, thinking about the changes in her own life lately. She walked around the counter and put Adele's latte on the table.

"Please, sit," Adele said, pointing to the chair across from her.

Molly sat down, a bit uncomfortable. She had never been great at meeting new people and making small talk, but she knew she had to get over that. Her big dream was to one day afford veterinary school and she'd definitely need to talk to new clients.

"So, you've only been in January Cove for a week or so? How are you liking it?"

"I love it, actually," Molly said with a smile. And she did love it, a lot more than she originally thought she would.

"It's a slice of heaven, for sure," Adele said with a proud smile. "It always feels good to come home again. There will never be another place like January Cove for me."

"Then why travel?"

"Well, I guess I'm just getting older and it's time to see some things. I spent most of my life raising kids and running a business, so it's nice to relax a little and see the world."

"And fall in love again?"

"Falling in love is the best feeling. You know, I lost my husband when my kids were young, and I adored him. It was the hardest day of my life, but my kids have made me so proud. And I know he would be thrilled with how they turned out."

"I love Addison. I'm staying at her B&B," Molly said.

"Oh, you are? That's a beautiful place. And Clay is a keeper too," Adele said with a laugh before taking a sip of her latte. "He's like another son to me since he practically lived at my house growing up."

"He seems like a great guy. Gotta find me one of those one day," Molly said with a sigh.

"Sounds like there's a story behind that sigh…"

"Yes, ma'am, but I'm too tired to tell it today," she said. Just then, a customer came into Jolt and gave Molly the break she needed from the line of questioning that was surely on its way. Adele was nice, but she could easily see how she'd raised five kids alone. She knew how to cross examine with grace and ease.

"Nice to meet you, Molly," Adele called, waving as she took her coffee out onto the sidewalk and Molly wondered how quickly she'd know her full story from Addison. She guessed within the next half hour, and that thought made her giggle to herself.

Small towns didn't even need newspapers. Gossip carried all the news quicker than social media ever could.

MOLLY ARRIVED home just before dinner. Rebecca had closed the coffee shop early in preparation for the rehearsal dinner for Aaron and Tessa's wedding the next day.

The dinner was being held at Breakers which meant that Addison and Clay were out for the night with Anna Grace. The whole family was getting together to toast the happy couple and run through the ceremony at the church nearby, which meant Molly was on her own for dinner.

She went up to her room, threw on some comfortable clothes - a pair of jeans and a long sleeved gray shirt - and went into the kitchen. Being alone in the big house was a little spooky, not because she believed in ghosts or anything, but because there were so many creaks and cracks and noises all the time. And, if an ax murderer suddenly appeared, she didn't know anyone to call for help.

"Hey," Austin said from behind, scaring the daylights out of her. Unfortunately, she had a knife in her hand at the time and swung around, flinging her arm up and narrowly missing his chin.

"Oh, I'm so sorry! Did I get you?" she asked, dropping the knife on the granite countertop and running her hand across his square jawline. The move sent unexpected tingles up her spine.

He cleared his throat and seemed a bit shaken by the event - or possibly her touching him - and stepped back. "Um, if you 'got me', we probably wouldn't be having this conversation right now."

She laughed. "Sorry. We seem to scare each other a lot."

"In more ways than one," he muttered as he opened the refrigerator.

"What?"

"Nothing. Where are Addison and Clay?"

"Oh, they had the rehearsal dinner tonight."

"So we're on our own?" he asked. She swore she heard a hopeful sound in his voice.

"I suppose so. I was just going to heat up a can of soup and watch TV in my room…"

"Dear God, are you an eighty year old woman? My grandma had a wilder social life."

"Excuse me?" she said, leaning against the counter and glaring at him.

"How old are you? Like twenty?"

"Twenty-two, actually."

"Oooh, sorry."

"Are you going back to being cocky, arrogant Austin because I can pick up that knife again." She loved their banter.

He studied her for a moment and then smiled. "No. I'm not going back. At least I'm not trying to go back, but it's hard. He's served me well for so many years."

She liked his crooked smile and that dimple that only showed on the right side, and only if he smiled big. Oh, no, what was she thinking?

"If he's served you so well, why aren't you already married off?" she asked innocently as she straightened up the bar stools lining the counter. It was a habit. Things had to be straight or she'd feel way too anxious.

He stopped what he was doing in the refrigerator - which seemed to be just letting the cold air out -

and looked at her. She couldn't pinpoint what his expression was. Anger? Hurt?

"If I wanted a wife, I'd have one," he said curtly and then turned toward the stairs.

"Oh come on! I was just messing around..." she said, following him.

"Stop," he said, holding his hand up. "Let's get something straight, Molly. We're friendly because we both live here right now. And I don't mind helping you find your sadistic catfish, but I don't owe you, or anyone else, explanations about my personal life. Understand?"

She just stood there, staring up at him in shock. The air was no longer in her lungs, and she felt a sense of horrible guilt washing over her. It was hurt, mixed with anger, that she saw in his eyes. But what had hurt him so bad that he lashed out at the least little comment?

AUSTIN SAT ON HIS BED, taking in deep breaths to calm himself down. He wasn't even mad at Molly; he was mad at himself. For what, he didn't really know.

A million times he'd questioned his choices. Not moving faster in his career. Not finding a wife and settling down. He always felt like he was running behind, like the last train had just left the station and he was chasing it. He had so much time he needed to catch up on, so many wasted years.

What she'd said had been innocent, and he had overreacted like he always did. She must've thought he was insane.

Maybe he should apologize, he thought, but apologies were hard for him. Vulnerability was impossible. People, especially women, couldn't be trusted. His own mother proved that.

So, he sat back on his bed and turned on the TV. Maybe he could find some kind of sporting event to get his mind off his troubles.

AUSTIN MUST HAVE DOZED off because he barely heard the knock at his door. It got louder and louder until he realized he wasn't dreaming.

"Come in," he called, still unable to focus his eyes. He glanced at his clock and realized an hour had passed, and then his stomach made an ungodly noise that reminded him he missed dinner.

The door swung open, as if being kicked, and Molly was standing there with a tray. On it were two bowls, two glasses of sweet tea and a plate of bread.

"Care to join me in my old woman dinner party?" she asked with a sly smile.

He laughed and nodded as he got up and took the tray from her. His room was a mess, at least compared to hers. Clothes were strewn all over the bed plus a few pieces on the floor. He put the tray down on his dresser and quickly tidied up as she stood there looking unsure of what to do.

"You need a maid."

"Are you offering?" he asked. She crossed her arms and cocked her head the side. "Here. Have a seat," he said, patting the bed. He pulled the bedside table between them and brought the food over.

"You know, we could go back to the table and eat this if you want."

"What? And ruin the ambiance in here? No way," he said.

She giggled and took a spoonful of her soup. It was homemade chicken soup, and Molly savored each bite like she'd never eaten before. It was a little hard to pay attention because he was so focused on watching her enjoy it.

"I'm really sorry for what I said earlier, Austin," she finally said, obviously trying to break the tension. He'd totally forgotten about their tiff in the kitchen, opting instead to focus on her lips.

Stop, he told himself.

"No biggie. I may have overreacted. Maybe. A little."

She chuckled. "No. Really? You? Unbelievable."

"So, tell me, Molly James… What was your life like back in Seattle?"

"Well, I didn't actually live in the city. We lived in a small town just outside of Seattle, but I worked there."

"At the veterinary clinic, right?"

"Yep."

"Do you miss it?" he asked, taking a big bite of bread like a hungry dog.

"I do. I love dogs. As soon as I can find a job working with animals again, I'll be so happy."

"And your parents? Do you miss them?"

She paused and looked down for a moment. It was obvious he'd hit a nerve. Maybe her parents weren't alive.

"Hard to say. I mean, I haven't been gone all that long." Her answer was short and almost sounded scripted. He wanted to know more, but he didn't press. "What about you? You grew up in Atlanta, right?"

"Yeah."

"Did you like it there?" she asked. He knew it was an innocent get-to-know-you type of question, but he hated talking about his upbringing. But for some reason, he was about to break one of his cardinal rules and he had no idea why.

"No. It wasn't a good time in my life," he said quietly.

"I'm sorry," she said. No prying. No questions.

"Don't you want to know why?"

"Only if you want me to know why," she said. Her voice was sweet, and he could've talked to her all night. That alone was making him nervous.

"I grew up on the wrong side of the tracks, so to speak. There were three of us kids. I was the oldest, but I have a younger brother and sister. My mom was a drug addict, and one day when I had just turned fifteen, she just left. Never saw her again."

She had stopped eating now. She was leaning across the small table, hanging on his every word.

"Oh, Austin. I know that must have been so hard on you…"

"We were split up," he continued, "and we all ended up in foster care. My siblings were fraternal twins and still in that cute phase." He smiled when he thought about them, all chubby faced and happy as babies. That hadn't lasted long. "They were adopted almost immediately. I have no idea where they are now."

"And you?"

"Foster care. Sent from place to place. Nobody wanted a punk teenage boy who was mad at the world. When I hit seventeen years old, I bolted. Ran away from the last place."

"They didn't care for you?"

"The mom was okay. The dad… well, let's just say he liked to use me as a punching bag."

Instinctively, she reached across the table and held his hand. He didn't move.

"Thank God, my best friend's Dad took me under his wing. He owns the development company I work for. So, the long answer to your question from before is that I've been so busy running from my past and trying to build a real life for myself that I've never had the chance to date much or look for a wife."

"Austin, it was just a joke. Honest. You're young with your whole life ahead of you."

"I just feel very behind," he said, standing up to get away from her hand touching his. It was just too much. The only problem was, she stood up too.

"Listen," she said, touching his arm and looking

up at him with those eyes, "you've got a bright future ahead of you. Anyone can see that. Your past doesn't have to define you."

"Thanks. And I'm sorry I'm ruining your old woman soup party," he said, breaking the ever-growing tension with a laugh.

She dropped her hand back to her side. "Hey, I saw more pudding downstairs. Wanna eat it before they get home?"

"I thought you'd never ask," he said, and he followed her out the door. And now his biggest problem was that he was pretty sure he'd follow her just about anywhere.

CHAPTER EIGHT

It was a beautiful morning in January Cove, and Tessa knew it was about to be the most changing day in her life. Of course, she and Tyler had lived with Aaron for a long time now, and she was making a wonderful home for them at Adele's old house, but this sealed the deal. They were officially, in the eyes of God and the law, going to become family today.

For what seemed like the hundredth time this morning, she dabbed a tissue over her eyes. She refused to have red, puffy eyes when she saw her groom standing at the altar in a couple of hours.

When she'd first shown up in January Cove, she had been terrified. On the run from her abusive ex, she and her two year old son at the time had been living in a crappy old camper in Crystal Cove Campground. And God knew way back then that Aaron Parker ran that campground and would save her from being scared ever again.

And he definitely had.

"Can I come in?" she heard her new mother-in-law call as she tapped on the door to the bridal room at the church. Tessa had gotten there super early hoping to calm her nerves and have some quiet time before walking down the aisle.

"Sure, come on in," Tessa said.

"Oh, you're such a beauty!" Adele said, grinning from ear to ear. It was funny, really, because she wasn't even wearing her wedding gown yet. She was wearing a simple white dress and very little makeup. Her hair stylist and makeup artist - better known as Addison - wouldn't be there for another thirty minutes.

"You're too sweet," Tessa said with a smile as she hugged Adele tightly. "I'm so glad you and Harrison made it here."

"We wouldn't have missed this for the world!" Adele said as she rubbed Tessa's arms. "Nervous?"

"Exceedingly," she said, being a little more verbose this morning than usual.

"Sweetie, Aaron is head over heels for you."

"I know. I just don't want to mess anything up. I want the service to be perfect."

"Oh Lord. Jenna didn't tell you her horror story, did she?" Adele asked with a pained look on her face.

"She did." The two women laughed.

"Pay her no mind. She has a terrible gag reflex," Adele said, waving her hand in front of her face. "You'll do fine."

"Adele, can I ask you something?"

"Of course, dear."

"Well, you know that I didn't exactly have the best life growing up. My mother passed away when I was just a little girl, and my father died in prison when I was just out of high school."

"I know. Terrible. I'm sure your momma would be so proud of you today." Adele always had reassuring words.

"I just wanted to ask… if it would be okay… to call you Mom?" Tessa had been wanting to ask Adele for months now because she was the only mother figure she'd had in so many years. She wanted that connection with another woman.

Adele's eyes welled with tears as a smile formed on her face. "I was so hoping you'd ask me that! Of course, sweetheart. I already think of you as my daughter anyway."

ADDISON WAS RUNNING around like a headless chicken. Having a baby and trying to get to Tessa's wedding venue was proving to be a bit of a challenge this morning.

"Clay? Have you seen the diaper bag?"

"I put it in my truck," he called back from upstairs.

"Good Lord! I've been looking everywhere for it!" she yelled up the stairs. She loved that man, but sometimes he tried to help without telling her what he was doing. Today was not the day for delays.

"Can I help with anything?" Molly said as she walked down the stairs and noticed Addison running around in a flurry of activity.

"Do you know how to do hair and makeup?"

"I'm pretty good with makeup. Why?"

"I think I need backup," Addison said with a smile. "Or do you already have plans for today?"

"Nope. No plans. But I don't want to intrude on the wedding…"

"Intrude? Honey, this is January Cove! Everyone is invited to everything."

Molly loved that. After her late night soup and pudding party with Austin, she was tired this morning, but she wasn't about to turn Addison's request for help down, especially since she didn't have to work.

"Well, then I'd love to come!" Molly said. She ran upstairs, threw on her nicest dress and heels and was back downstairs in minutes. Clay kept the baby at home while the two women drove to the church.

"I just love weddings," Addison said smiling as she drove. "So much hope and happiness in one room."

"Me too. I've only been to a couple, though."

"Well, you're young. I'm sure yours will be coming soon," Addison said.

"Not even close!"

"You never know. Miracles always happen when you least expect them. I never expected Clay to be my soulmate. I'd known him my whole life, but God sometimes has other plans."

Molly had no idea what plan God had for her life, but she knew for sure it didn't involve a guy named Blake.

By the time Addison and Molly arrived, Tessa was pacing the room.

"Finally!" she said to Addison. She looked at Molly for a moment with a confused face.

"Sorry. Clay didn't tell me where the diaper bag was and then I had to give it back to him and Anna Grace is still getting over her ear infection and…"

"And you are?" Tessa said, ignoring Addison's rambling as she reached her hand out to Molly.

"Oh, I'm sorry. This is Molly. She's staying at the B&B and is going to help me get your makeup perfect."

"Nice to meet you, Molly. Sorry if I seemed abrupt. Today is just… hectic. Anxiety producing…"

"No problem. I totally understand. Your dress is stunning." Molly stood in front of the long white gown that was hanging in the corner of the room. It was a real princess dress with jewels encrusted on the bodice and a long veil.

As a little girl, she used to dream of a real white knight coming to rescue her, only he was on a zebra. She was always an odd kid.

Her perfect dress had a hoop inside it to make it stick out just like the dresses that Scarlett O'Hara wore, but maybe that wasn't quite in fashion these days.

"Thank you. It was way over my budget, but you only get married once, right? Actually, twice I guess.

Oh well, who's counting?" Tessa was obviously anxious, talking a mile a minute as she buzzed about the room doing absolutely nothing productive.

"Well, congratulations," Molly said with a smile. Tessa was definitely a beautiful woman with her darker toned skin and blue eyes. She was going to look beautiful in her dress for sure.

"Thanks. I feel like I've been waiting for this day for my whole life," she said. Addison put her arm around Tessa's shoulders.

"And I know my brother has too." Tessa grinned from ear to ear.

"I can't wait to be Mrs. Tessa Parker. And I can't wait to change Tyler's name too."

"Where is Tyler?"

"He's with Adele now. I swear that kid has been passed around all day long!"

"I'm sure he's fine," Addison said. "Now, let's get started on making you even more beautiful!"

MOLLY TOOK a seat in the back of the small white church. Both sides were filling up, although Addison had told her that Tessa didn't have family coming. In fact, Jackson would be walking Tessa down the aisle as the eldest Parker brother.

Coming from such a judgmental family, Molly had never seen siblings so close. The whole town seemed that way, as if time stood still in January Cove.

She felt someone slide in beside her, the smell of cologne floating past her before she saw who it was.

"Hey," Austin whispered, and she got a chill again. Not good.

"What're you doing here?"

"Clay asked me to come. He's going to need some help setting up for the reception later."

"Oh."

The service started seconds later, and Molly reached down to silence her phone. She noticed a text message.

You haven't responded to my texts lately. I miss you. Did I do something to upset you?

It was "Fake Blake" as she'd come to call him. She'd successfully avoided his texts since getting the news that he wasn't who he said he was, but mainly because she didn't know what to say.

Austin reached for her phone and read the text.

"Um, excuse me. Nosy!" she whispered loudly into his ear.

"He's seriously still texting you? Here, let me respond."

"No!"

"Molly," he whispered, "we don't want to tip him off that we're on to him. Come on. Let me…"

She handed him the phone and he quickly typed something in and handed it back.

I miss you too. Just a little busy with a big family issue. I'll be in touch soon. Smooches!

The bridesmaids started filing in as music filled the church.

"Smooches? Really? I would never say that."

"Oh? What would you say then?" he whispered.

"I don't know. Maybe 'kisses'?"

Austin chuckled. Someone shushed him as the Wedding March started playing.

The back doors of the church opened revealing Tessa in her gorgeous gown. She took Jackson's arm and made her way down the aisle. Molly leaned over to see her train, the back of her hair blocking Austin's view. She could've sworn he sniffed her hair, but there was no way to prove it.

She sat back, gave him a weird look and focused her attention on the front of the church.

"We are gathered together…" the pastor started. Molly tuned out as she looked around at all of the smiling January Cove residents. They were like a picture postcard of a place she'd wanted to visit all of her life. Happy people. Welcoming people. It already felt like a home, a place she actually belonged. A place where people just accepted her for who she was.

"Let us join hands and pray..." Suddenly, Austin was holding her hand, but then so was the woman next to her. All she could feel was his warm, strong hand. It was nice. He had his eyes closed and head bowed. Maybe she should do the same. At least that's what she was thinking when he opened his eyes and caught her looking at him. She quickly closed her eyes and then the moment was over. He let go of her hand and a void was there now, which only confused her.

The wedding vows were the most beautiful part of the ceremony, at least to Molly. In fact, there didn't seem to be a dry eye in the place - well, except for Austin. Apparently, his tear ducts were made of steel and were under lock and key.

Molly could only hear parts and pieces of the vows, but it was enough to make her long for a love like that. Unconditional love from a man who accepted her, faults and all.

"You were the man who saved me and my son from a

life spent hiding. When everyone else ran away, you ran toward us, arms open wide and ready to accept us. I can never thank you enough or say I love you enough for everything you do for us and everything you are as a person," Tessa said, tears flowing down her cheeks.

"Every dream I ever had for my life is wrapped up in you, Tessa. There is no one on this Earth that I'd rather spend my life with, and I promise I will protect you and Tyler every day for the rest of my life," she heard Aaron say.

It was wonderful, inspiring and utterly depressing.

When the wedding was over, Austin slipped out to help Clay and Molly was left there longing for a love like that. Longing to touch Austin's hand again. She mentally slapped away the thought.

The reception was one big party at a large plantation house about a block away. It was a lovely home, bigger than the B&B, and it was packed. Many people who weren't at the wedding - probably because they couldn't fit in the tiny church - showed up for the reception, and the whole town seemed to be in attendance. Even the mayor was there.

"Having fun?" Austin asked as he walked up beside her. The music blared from the DJ booth, and people moved around the dance floor.

"Oh sure. Standing alone in a room full of strangers is a total blast," she said with a sarcastic smile.

"I'm not a stranger. I've eaten massive amounts of soup with you and now we've held hands."

His dry humor was growing on her. "Yeah. We're besties now!" she yelled over a particularly loud Taylor Swift song.

"Do you dance?" he yelled back.

"What?"

"Do you dance?" he repeated. She'd heard him the first time, but needed to buy herself a few moments before answering.

"Not usually!" she yelled back.

"Oh, come on!" He grabbed her hand yet again and pulled her to the dance floor. Being petite sucked when it came to fighting back in situations like this. They started to dance, but the song suddenly changed and it slowed way down. Oh no. Awkward….

"Um…" Molly said as she started to back off the dance floor.

Instead, inexplicably, Austin reached for her hand and pulled her close. He slid one hand around her waist and took her other hand in his. For a moment, he stood there and just stared deep into her eyes as if he was silently asking for permission to pull her closer.

She couldn't speak. He smelled good. He was warm. He was hot. What was a girl to do?

AUSTIN SWAYED TO THE MUSIC, struggling to understand his own thoughts. She was backing off the dance floor, and then he basically grabbed her? *Smooth move, dummy. She probably thinks you're a pervert now, grabbing her like that.*

And why did he pull her back? They could have walked right off the floor, no harm no foul. But no, he had to show his cards right then and there.

He wanted to hold her in his arms. He almost hadn't let go of her hand in the church, and he wondered if she noticed that he held hers a few seconds longer even after the preacher stopped praying?

And now he was in a sticky situation. He was holding this woman, this goddess-like creature who smelled like lavender and coffee mixed together, and he was struggling with every feeling, emotion and thought.

This couldn't happen. *They* couldn't happen. His

carefully laid plans were starting to backfire. January Cove was just a pitstop on the way to a big, bold, successful life. And this petite little auburn-haired beauty had not been in his plans at all.

Plus, she was too gullible and innocent for a guy like him. He'd end up hurting her by saying or doing something stupid. He was too cocky and arrogant for her. She deserved better. Not a catfish and not him, but none of those thoughts stopped him from pulling her even closer until her head was rested against his chest.

Oh good Lord. This was an accident waiting to happen.

YEP, her head was firmly on his chest. His cologne was unbelievably alluring, and she was having a hard time keeping her eyes open. She just wanted to bask in the moment of being held by this gorgeous man.

Please let the next song be fast, she thought to herself. And yet she knew she didn't really want that. She wanted every song to be a slow song until everyone else got bored and left her, swaying back and forth, with Austin until the sun came up.

It could happen, right?

And then the song was over. Why are songs so dang short?

They continued swaying for a moment until the floor was covered up in people doing the Electric Slide. Austin cleared his throat and stepped back, opening the space between them and creating yet another void.

"Thanks for the dance," she said softly. Somehow he heard her over the music and nodded.

"Ditto."

"I'm really tired. I think I'm going to head back to the B&B now."

"Mind if I walk with you?" he asked. She nodded, they said their goodbyes to everyone and headed out the door.

CHAPTER NINE

I t was a cool late October evening, and January Cove was already lit up for the holidays that were coming in less than eight weeks. It seemed like it was a place that was just made for Christmas with its beautiful architecture and moonlit views of the water.

As Austin and Molly walked, they were quiet at first. Her heels were killing her, and she just wanted to get home.

"Can I ask you something?" Austin said, immediately making Molly's stomach clench up.

"Sure..." she said, holding the word out.

"What did your parents say about you coming all the way out here to meet Fake Blake?" She loved that he'd accepted her new nickname of the catfish.

"Ohhhh.... That's a story in itself. They weren't happy. Of course, they aren't happy about most things I do."

"Really? Seems like you have it pretty together to me." She knew it was just an off the cuff comment, but it made her feel validated. At least someone thought nice things about her.

"Thanks, but I obviously don't. I mean, I followed a stranger across the country. You said so yourself." He reached over and stopped her.

"And I apologized for that."

"I know. I'm not mad or anything."

Austin pointed to a small bench on near the square. They sat down which was a welcome rest for her aching feet.

"The more I think about it, the more I admire you for what you did."

"Really?"

"Yeah. You took a chance for love. You just took that chance on the wrong person," he said. There was a tone in his voice that she couldn't quite place.

"Well, I feel like a total fool." She looked up at the sky. The moon was almost full, and the stars were plentiful, although they were harder to see with the street lights around them.

"You're no fool, Molly James," he said softly.

"You're a little obsessed with banana pudding, but you're not a fool."

"Me? What about you?" she said, playfully smacking his arm.

They stood up and started walking again, but Molly finally ditched her shoes and held them in her hand.

"So, any siblings?" he asked.

"One very perfect brother on the path to being the next Bill Gates."

"Ouch."

"Yeah. I didn't quite measure up. Dyslexic. Homely. Awkward."

"Stop!" he said, spinning her toward him. He looked flustered and upset, but she had no idea why.

"What's wrong?" she asked, looking around wondering if a car had been careening toward them or something.

"You have to stop saying that crap. God, Molly, what have your parents done to you? It's like you're brainwashed against yourself."

"It's hard to argue with the truth, Austin."

"But it's not the truth. You're not homely. You're stunning. That auburn hair, most girls would kill for that color, but you just have it naturally. It's like you have glints of sunlight," he said, reaching up and touching a strand of her hair. "And your eyes are the most amazing shade of emerald green. I've never seen anyone with the color of your eyes." He was speaking so softly, and the streets were deserted with only the faint sound of the ocean waves a block away. Only in January Cove could they stand in the middle of the road without worrying about a car coming.

"I... don't..." she stammered. No one had ever said those things to her, not even Fake Blake.

"You don't need to say anything," he said, dropping his hand to his side and stepping back. "You just need to know that you're perfect exactly like you are. Soup and all."

Austin seemed to always fall back on his dry sense of humor to get out of tough emotional spots, and this definitely seemed like one of them.

They started walking again and the B&B finally came into view. It was a welcome sight as far as her feet were concerned, but she kind of wanted to spend the night walking every street in January Cove with Austin by her side.

"Thank you, Austin."

"For what?" he asked as they started up the walkway to the B&B.

"For everything."

AUSTIN COULDN'T GET to his room quick enough. What was this woman doing to him? Soon, he'd be reciting poetry and painting with watercolors in the garden.

But he couldn't help it. She was downgrading herself, and it wasn't right. He'd probably never meet her parents, but he had to wonder what kind of people they were to have not appreciated such an amazing daughter.

Still, he had to keep his distance. He wasn't her knight in shining armor. He wasn't that kind of guy. He was focused on his own goals, his own dreams. Only now he was totally confused on exactly what his dreams were.

"OKAY, that's seriously the cutest thing I've ever seen!" Molly said with a grin as Addison carried Anna Grace into Jolt wearing her Halloween costume. She was dressed as a puppy dog with a cute brown nose painted on.

"Isn't she adorable? Of course, I'm a bit biased," Addison said with a smile. Jolt was about to close for the day, so Molly made Addison a quick hot chocolate.

"Getting ready to trick or treat?"

"Yes. This will be her first time, and I know she won't remember a bit of it, but I'm having fun reliving my own childhood all over again!"

"Where's Clay?"

"Oh, he's at home getting ready to hand out candy to the kids. We expect a lot of them."

"Why isn't he going with you? Surely he wants to see Anna Grace trick or treat for the first time."

"He does, but we can't leave the B&B unattended on a night like this! We might get egged," she said with a laugh. That would probably never happen in January Cove.

"Let me hand out candy! I'm leaving here in a few minutes, and I'd love to help out," Molly said as she tickled Anna Grace's feet and watched her squirm and giggle.

"Are you sure? I don't want to impose or interfere on any of your plans?"

"Plans? I have no plans, Addy," she said. It was sad, but true.

"Well… if you don't mind…"

"I'll be home shortly." Molly smiled and waved as Addison walked out, holding her adorable daughter, and she wondered if one day she'd have a daughter of her own to do the same things with.

One thing was for sure - if she ever did have a daughter, she'd love and accept her for who she was.

MOLLY CARRIED the three huge buckets of candy into the foyer, ready for the onslaught of kids that would soon be knocking.The sun was about to go down, and she expected the doorbell to ring any second.

When it did, she swung it open with a big smile.

"Happy Halloween!" she exclaimed, but it wasn't trick or treaters. It was her parents.

"Mom? Dad? What are you doing here?"

"We came to see our daughter, of course," her mother said with a plastered on smile. She reached for Molly and gave her a quick hug before moving past her and into the house. Her father followed with his own version of a quick embrace and moved inside too, leaving Molly standing there with a bucket of candy. She wondered how far she could get before they'd catch her in a foot race.

She closed the door, after taking a quick peek up the street to make sure no kids were coming, and placed the bucket next to the door on a table.

Her parents stood there expectantly, luggage in hand. Not a good sign.

"I don't understand. Why didn't you tell me you were coming?"

"You haven't exactly been responding to my texts, dear," her mother said with that look on her face. Molly had seen that look all her life. Disapproval, plain and simple.

"I've been busy with work and some other things. Come on in," Molly said, walking them into the kitchen. Her parents both sat down at the kitchen table, but her mother looked extremely uncomfortable as she surveyed the place like it was a truck stop or homeless shelter.

"So, this is where you've chosen to live?" her mother said, the snideness in her voice apparent. "It's very… Southern."

"Temporarily. It's a bed and breakfast, mother. And it's been lovely. The people who run this place are the salt of the Earth."

"And where are they?"

"Trick or treating with their daughter. You kind of picked a bad night to arrive," Molly said, but she was interrupted by the doorbell. She walked to the door, gave the kids candy, complimented their adorable costumes - which ranged from Superman to some kind of zombie - and returned to her parents.

"Molly, we came to ask you to come home with us." Her father's no nonsense approach was at least refreshing from her mother's beat around the bush concept, but she wasn't going anywhere.

"And why would I do that?"

"Because this place isn't for you. It's so far from Seattle, and what kind of job prospects could you possibly have here?" her mother said.

"Well, I work at the coffee shop, and I like it. I'm thinking about starting a dog walking business in the spring when the tourists arrive..."

"Dog walking?" Her mother looked like she was holding off on gagging. "Oh, Molly..."

"Honestly, Mother, you act like I just told you I had the plague or something."

"What kind of life is this?" her mother asked, looking around the room. The B&B was beautiful. Quaint. Southern. Molly looked around the room too, trying desperately to see anything wrong. But with her mother, nothing had to be wrong - she could still judge it just fine.

"It's a good life." Molly stood up and handed out candy once more, listening to her mother sigh as she got up.

"Don't they have someone who could do that?" she called behind her.

"Do what?"

"Hand out candy."

"I offered."

"They're taking advantage of your naiveté, dear," her mother said when she returned to the table. Molly decided to stand since the doorbell was going to ring over and over again.

"No, they're not. Look, this is a place that thrives on family."

"They're not your family, Molly. These people are perfect strangers!"

"No, they're not! They've become like family to me already. They accept me, and they listen to me."

"And what about the infamous Blake? Huh? Where is he?"

"I…. Um…"

"Right. Just like I thought. He doesn't even exist, does he? I knew it! I tried to tell you…"

"Hey, sweetie," Molly heard Austin say from behind. She looked at him, totally confused and started to speak. But instead, he put his index finger over her lips and kissed her neck, sending chills up and down her body. "Play along…" he murmured into her ear.

"Who are you?" Molly's mother demanded.

"I'm Blake. Nice to meet you, finally," he said, reaching over and shaking both of her parents' hands as they sat there stunned. Austin was dressed to impress for some reason, wearing a nice pair of dark wash jeans and a button up pale pink shirt. "Molly has told me so much about you over the last year."

"Yes… um… she's told us a lot about you too…" her father stammered.

Inside, Molly was giddy with excitement. Austin had just bailed her out of a really sticky situation. Now her parents would have no choice but to get on the first plane back to Washington.

"So, how long are you staying in January Cove?" Austin asked as he sat down on the bar stool and pulled Molly backward by her waist. He situated her on his knee and rested his head on her left shoulder. She hoped that he couldn't feel her shaking and quivering all over.

"Maybe a few weeks," her mother said. Molly almost choked.

"What? Why?" Molly said, a little too loudly and at a higher octave than she intended.

"Don't you want us here, Molly?" her mother asked, a hurt tone in her voice.

"Well… Of course… But doesn't Daddy have to work?"

"I took a few weeks off. Doctor's orders." He rolled his eyes as far back into his head as possible.

"Oh, God. Is everything okay?"

"He'll be fine. Your father's blood pressure was a little too high, so his doctor recommended some much needed time off," her mother explained. She carefully watched Molly and Austin as he hugged her closer and kissed her cheek.

"Well, sweetie, I've got that business dinner to get to. Walk me out?"

"Business? What kind of business?" her father asked, his eyes furrowed together.

"Real estate development. I work for the largest development company in the Southeast. Ballard. Maybe you've heard of it?"

"Yes, I have, actually. Mac Ballard owns that, right?"

Molly's insides were tightening up. How did her father know that?

"Yes, sir."

"I'm in the financial planning world. Heard a lot about Mac over the years."

"He's a great man," Austin said as he stood. "See you soon."

Molly followed Austin into the yard, handing out more candy before they left the porch. He pulled her behind the large oak tree where they could be in a quiet, dark place away from her parents and any kids.

"Why did you do that, Austin?" she asked softly.

"Because you needed me to," he said. "I couldn't listen to them batter you anymore."

Her heartbeat quickened. "But they could be here for weeks. How are we going to keep up this charade?"

"Well, first of all, you're going to have to start calling me Blake. And you'd better forewarn Addison and Clay too."

"I will…"

"And we'll have to pretend date."

"And that's why you kissed my neck and my cheek and sat me on your lap?" she asked, a coy smile on her face.

"That's my story and I'm sticking to it," he said as he started to walk away.

"Austin?"

"Yeah?"

"Thank you."

He winked and walked down the sidewalk, and

Molly was left wondering how they were going to pull this off.

AUSTIN STOPPED AROUND THE CORNER, just out of sight, and took a deep breath. He watched through the trees as Molly walked back up to the porch and into the B&B.

What had he just done? The whole thing was completely insane. Pretend to be her boyfriend - by a whole different name - for the next few weeks all while trying to build a restaurant and not lose his job? Oh, and trying to find her catfish who started this whole mess in the first place?

This was a can of worms that was better left closed, but had he listened to his head? Nope. In fact, the moment he'd heard her parents talking to her that way, he'd struggled not to walk around the corner and throw both of her parents out on their butts.

But, as his grandmother used to say, he could catch more flies with honey. Was that even true? And why would anyone be catching flies in the first place?

Realizing he was getting mentally off track, he

started walking again. Tonight he had a big meeting with an investor. Mac Ballard had called asking him to meet the guy because he was tied up, so this was Austin's chance to show his stuff.

The only problem right now was he couldn't get the smell of Molly's hair out of his nose, and he couldn't stop reliving her sitting on his knee either.

Women were nothing but trouble.

"ADDISON AND CLAY, these are my parents, Lydia and George James," Molly said, a pained smile on her face as she introduced her parents. "They surprised me tonight, but I still managed to hand out all the candy."

"So nice to meet you both," Addison said, reaching out to shake their hands and smiling brightly. She had an innate sense of making people feel comfortable. Nothing like her family who seemed to delight in making everyone around them uncomfortable.

"Good to meet you. I hope you have a room for us?" Molly suddenly realized that her parents intended to stay there. At the B&B. With her... and Austin.

Oh, no. How was this ever going to work? They'd be watching her every move, and Austin's too. Maybe she needed to just come clean.

"Of course. We have a lovely room at the other end of the hallway from Molly. It's been fully renovated. How long do you plan to stay with us?" Addison asked.

"Maybe a few weeks. At least through Thanksgiving," her mother said.

Thanksgiving? What? Oh no. This was bad bad bad.

"Mom, surely you and Dad want to have Thanksgiving at home."

"Why? Your brother will be on a trip, and you're out here... chasing your text message boyfriend. At least you found him and he doesn't seem like an ax murderer."

Addison looked at Molly with confusion.

"Yes, Mom, Blake is a wonderful guy. But let's talk about that later. I'm sure Addison and Clay are ready to get Anna Grace settled in for the night..." Molly urged as she pushed her mother toward the stairs.

"Here, let me help you with those bags," Clay said, handing Anna Grace off to Addison and leading her parents up the stairs.

"I'll be up in a minute," Molly called to them and then turned her attention to a very confused Addison.

"Okay, what's going on?"

"Not a lot of time to explain, but the nutshell version is that my parents showed up without notice and started hounding me about whether Blake was real or not. I was just about to tell them the truth when Austin appeared from nowhere and pretended to be Blake. So now we're pretend dating."

Addison looked thoroughly confused and overwhelmed with the quick update. "Pretend dating?"

"Yes. For a few weeks."

"And don't you think it will look strange that he's living here in the B&B?"

Molly hadn't considered that, and neither had Austin, she assumed. If he was going to his own room at night, that would make no sense as he was supposed to live local.

"Crap. I hadn't even thought of that."

"Look, if you want this to work, Austin needs to stay in your room, at least when your parents are around."

Molly felt flush. Austin staying in her room? That sounded like a very bad idea… and a very good one at the same time.

CHAPTER TEN

Molly paced her room waiting for Austin to come back to the B&B. He'd been gone for at least two hours, and she felt a pang of jealousy when she realized he could actually be out on a date or something.

Thankfully, her parents had gone to bed, worn out by a day of traveling, so she had some time to make a plan. Either they would work this out or she'd have to come clean.

She heard footsteps coming up the stairs and peeked out her door to see Austin unlocking the door to his room.

"Psst!" she said in a loud whisper. Austin was startled to find her standing there waving her hand wildly. "Come here!"

She opened her door, grabbed his arm and jerked him inside.

"Hey, that's no way to greet your pretend boyfriend!" he said with a chuckle.

"Not funny. We have a problem." She closed the door quietly behind her.

"What kind of problem?"

"Addison pointed out a hole in your plan."

"Oh now it's *my* plan?"

"Well, pretty boy, you did jump into this all by yourself."

"True. And don't call me pretty. Call me hot, sexy, stud muffin…"

"Can you please pay attention?"

"I'm trying, but you're kind of taking a long time to get to the point." Again, he was a funny guy but now wasn't the time.

"You're going to have to stay in my room until my parents leave town."

Austin's eyes got wide and a smile slowly spread across his face. "Got the hots for your pretend boyfriend, do ya?"

She wasn't sure what the answer was, but she wasn't about to admit to anything. "My parents know that Blake lives locally, so why would he have a room at a B&B?"

Austin sat down and took in the info for a moment. "Very true, and obviously Addison is way smarter than either of us. So you basically want your parents to think you're shacking up in this room with me?"

"Not the way I would've phrased it, but I guess so. Now what are we going to do?"

"Like you said, I need to stay here."

Molly looked at him for a moment. "I'm not sure that's a good idea."

Austin stood and crossed the room, his face leaned into hers with only an inch between them. "Why, Molly? Worried you can't keep your hands off of me?"

"Have you been drinking or something?" she asked, her arms crossed.

"Maybe."

"Well, get real, buddy, because I can totally keep my hands off of you. And you're sleeping on the sofa over there. The bed is mine."

Austin sighed and walked to the door. "I think I'm getting the raw end of this deal. I'm paying for a room, but I get to sleep on the sofa over here. Terrible deal…" he muttered as he walked across the hall to get a few things.

A NIGHT on the sofa had proven to suck even more than Austin thought. Not only did he have to see Molly walk around her room wearing a nightshirt, but he had to keep his hands to himself and sleep on the world's hardest couch.

Still, he found himself wanting to be near her. It didn't matter the place or situation, he enjoyed her company. They picked at each other, and she got his weird humor.

They'd had breakfast together with her parents, and he'd withstood their onslaught. In fact, her father seemed to be warming up, asking him lots of questions about real estate development. And to Austin's surprise, he could answer most of them which made him feel like he was finally getting somewhere in his career.

The dinner with the investor had gone well, and he was pretty sure Ballard would be delighted with what he'd done. All in all, life was getting better in January Cove. Better than he could've ever imagined.

"Knock knock!" he heard a voice say as he sat in the trailer going over spreadsheets. The door opened and his best friend, Eddie, appeared.

"Dude! What are you doing here?" Austin jumped up and bear hugged his friend, so happy to see a familiar face.

"Thought I'd make a surprise visit!"

"Lots of those around here lately," Austin muttered under his breath.

"Huh?"

"Oh, nothing. It's so good to see you, man!"

"I hope you've got a place for me to stay while I'm here?"

Austin froze. "Well... let me tell you the situation..."

He spent the next several minutes detailing all of it, from meeting Molly to her parents showing up and having to move in with her.

"So let me get this straight," Eddie said, leaning back in the chair across from Austin's desk and putting his feet up, "you don't care about this chick, but you rode in like a knight in shining armor and saved her from her evil parents?"

"I wouldn't exactly put it that way."

"Oh my gosh. I never thought I'd live to see the day."

"What day?"

"Austin York falling in love." Eddie beamed with

pride and pretended to wipe away a tear from his eyes.

"I am not in love. I'm just helping a friend, that's it," Austin said as he stood up and pulled a file from the filing cabinet in the corner of the room.

"I've known you for a long time, Austin. You can't play me."

"Eddie, cut it out. Seriously," Austin said, leaning over the chair, his hands turning white with the force of pressure he was holding on to the arm of the chair.

"Calm down. I'm happy for you, man. That's all. You deserve this."

"I don't deserve *her*," Austin said as he stood back up.

"And why is that?"

"Come on, man. You know me. You know my past and my personality. No woman like her is ever going to choose a man like me."

"You mean a hard working guy who rides up on his white horse and saves the day?"

"That's not me."

Eddie stood up and faced his friend, putting his hands on Austin's shoulders.

"Listen up. You're not that fifteen year old kid

anymore. You're a man, and you've changed a lot over the years. When are you going to stop punishing yourself for having a rough life back then?"

"I just don't feel…"

"Worthy of her. I get it. But you are, Austin. You're in control of your life now. When are you going to accept that and move on?"

It was a good question. The only problem was, he didn't have an answer.

MOLLY SAT IN HER ROOM, taking a momentary respite away from her parents. Rebecca had given her the whole day off so she could show her parents around January Cove, which she did. And that's why she was now hiding in her room.

She showed them Jolt, which her mother criticized for not having big enough tables. She showed them the beach, which her mother criticized for not having enough seashells. And then she showed them the ferry, which her mother described as a "rickety dock with a rusted out boat".

It had been exhausting.

Her father, as usual, didn't say much and checked his email every five minutes, making several business calls throughout the day. And when her brother called their father to tell them about his new promotion, that's all they could talk about for the rest of the day so Molly brought them back.

She decided that a nice, long bath was in order, even if it was just five in the afternoon. Maybe it would calm her down enough to eat dinner with them later.

She filled the tub with hot water and as many bubbles as it would fit and slid into it with her headphones blaring Maroon 5 songs.

When she opened her eyes again, Austin was staring back at her.

"What are you doing in here?" she yelped, looking down to make sure the bubbles were covering all the right places. Thank goodness they were.

"You left the door open. And then I realized you were asleep, so I didn't want you to drown," he said, but she couldn't help but notice that he was smiling.

"Can you… go?" she asked, waving toward the door.

"But I need to talk to you."

"Well, I'd rather talk with my clothes on."

"Are you sure?"

"Get out!" she said, throwing a mound of bubbles at him.

A few minutes later, she was back in her clothes and ready to talk. Austin was sitting on her bed, leafing through a women's magazine and chuckling to himself.

"Do you ladies really take these silly quizzes?"

"Give me that. What do you want to talk about?" she said, swiping the magazine from his hands and throwing it on the dresser.

"I've got news on your catfish."

"What? How?"

"I've been doing a little behind the scenes work."

"Okay…"

"I spoke with the guy who lives in the house you went to. He's lived there for fifteen years."

"I already knew that."

"But did you know he's rented the place for the summer once or twice while he traveled himself?"

"No, I didn't know that…"

"Well, he rented it last summer, right around the time you met Fake Blake."

"What? Why didn't he tell me that?" she asked,

irritated that the man had kept the information from her.

"I don't know. I guess he didn't think about it. Anyway, he actually rented it twice, for two weeks each time. Here's the names of the people who rented it," Austin said, handing it to Molly. "Recognize any of those names?"

Molly looked at the piece of paper. The first renter was Hillary Callahan, and the second renter was Wilton Marshall.

"I don't recognize either name," she said, disappointed that the answer wasn't staring her in the face.

"Dang. I was hoping it would be as easy as that. We'll have to keep digging. Are you still getting texts from him?"

"Everyday. I usually make a quick response or ignore, but I think he knows something is up."

Austin smiled.

"What?"

"You don't tear up anymore when you talk about him."

He was right. She didn't feel anything anymore when she got a text from him. In fact, she wished he would stop texting altogether. She would've already changed her number except she wanted to find the guy and crush him under the soles of her shoes.

"It doesn't bother me anymore," she said as she pulled her knees up to her chest and leaned against her pillow.

"Why?"

"I don't know. I guess I've moved on to bigger things."

There was an awkward silence in the room for a moment.

"Well, at least you moved up from a fake boyfriend to a pretend one."

"At least I can reach out and touch my pretend boyfriend," she said, giggling as she reached out and touched his forearm. Much to her shock, he grabbed her hand and held it against his arm for a moment before letting go.

"Um, Addison told me to see if you're ready for dinner?"

"Yeah. Sure. I just need to put my shoes on..."

Molly stood up and slipped on her black flats as Austin opened the door. When they walked into the hallway, her parents were just coming out of their room.

"Ready for dinner?" Molly asked.

Her mother was dressed to the nines, which seemed a bit much for a family dinner.

"Yes. We have reservations for four at Bel Cibo in thirty minutes."

"But, Mom, I think Addison is cooking dinner."

"Good grief, Molly, do we have to eat here for every meal? I think we've been very congenial with your hosts here, but must we spend all of our time in this place?"

"Mom…"

"Relax, sweetie. I'll make our regrets to Addison and meet you outside, okay?" Austin said with a forced smile.

Molly nodded and followed her parents downstairs to her rental car.

"Molly, dear, I have a question for you," her mother said when they got outside.

"What?" Molly was exhausted and her parents had only been there a couple of days.

"I haven't seen you kiss Blake one time."

"That's not a question, Mother."

"Well, I was just expecting a little more romance between you two seeing as you were so head over heels in love," she said with a definite sarcastic tone. "Trouble in paradise?"

"No, of course not! I just didn't think you'd want to see me all over some guy."

"Well, if he's living in your room and about to become your husband, then I would expect to see some evidence of your undying love for each other," she said, pursuing her lips. It was apparent that her mother wasn't completely falling for her pretend boyfriend act. She had to do something.

Austin walked down the stairs toward the car and smiled. "Addison totally understood."

Before he could say more, Molly turned around. "Thank you for telling her, honey. I'm the luckiest girl in the world to have you as my future husband," she said, and then she did the craziest thing she'd ever done. She reached her hands around his neck, pulled his lips to hers and kissed him like her life depended on it.

At first, it was for show, but then something happened. Something she didn't expect. The whole world vanished, went black and all that existed were her and Austin. The warmth of his lips, the eagerness of his tongue slipping into her mouth, his hands around her waist pulling her closer. She felt herself melting into him and then...

"Molly! Please! That's enough!" her mother shouted. Molly mentally checked herself to be sure all of her clothes were still on, and she could feel her face flush with redness. Was it embarrassment or heat? She had no idea.

When she finally turned around, her mother was visibly angry, but she said nothing more and got into the car. Molly turned back to Austin who looked more stunned than anything.

"I'm sorry," she whispered. "They weren't buying it. I had to take it up a notch."

Austin walked around to open the passenger side door for her and whispered back, "Did you hear me complain?"

AS AUSTIN DROVE, he was quiet, allowing Molly's parents to give the latest update on her brother, Liam. All he could think about was that kiss. That amazing kiss. He'd kissed a good number of women in his time, but nothing like that.

He hadn't expected it, and he hadn't wanted it to stop. He'd forgotten all time and space until Molly's mother had yelled at them. He'd never been so close to strangling a woman, but he'd considered it for a split second when he felt the void of her lips on his.

In the end, he knew she was only playing a part.

He was basically an actor, and actors kissed actresses all the time without falling in love. He could certainly do the same.

Only he wasn't an actor. And this was getting out of hand.

THEY ARRIVED at the restaurant and were seated at a table overlooking the beach. It was a beautiful evening, the sunset painting pink streaks across the ever darkening sky. Molly could smell the salt water in the air, and the ocean waves roared in like clockwork.

After they ordered, the waiter invited them to enjoy the dance floor. A jazz band was playing on the patio, so Molly's parents excused themselves for a dance which gave Austin and Molly a chance to talk.

"I'm so sorry, again, for springing that kiss on you," she said softly. He reached under the table and took her hand. "You know they can't see your hand, right?" she asked with a smile.

"I know." And yet he continued holding her hand. Finally, after a few moments, he asked her to dance. They walked out to the dance floor, hand in hand.

Austin slipped both of his hands around her waist as she reached around his neck. They were close now, almost as close as when they kissed, and she could feel someone's heart pounding. Whether it was hers or his, she had no idea, but the energy between them was almost electric.

He pulled her closer, giving her no other option but the rest her cheek against his chest. Yep, it was his heartbeat, although hers was keeping time with his. He smelled so good. She wanted to bury her nose in his shirt, but that might get them kicked out.

He was holding her so tightly, resting his chin on the top of her head. She felt safer than she ever had in her life in that moment, even though she knew the whole thing was an act. Honestly, she wondered if Austin had taken acting classes at some point because their kiss had been magical.

Her parents, mostly her mom, were watching them closely, looking for any reason to trip them up. She had no idea why her mother was so suspicious, but it was obvious that she was.

"They've brought our drinks," her mother said as she tapped Molly on the shoulder. Molly hummed a response and kept swaying with her eyes closed for a few moments longer as her parents made their way back to the table.

"I guess we'd better go back," Austin whispered as he continued moving back and forth, pulling her closer if that was even possible. She hugged him tightly, nuzzling her face into his chest and sighing. Oh God, did he hear her sigh?

"Yeah..." she said. It was so comfortable, so perfect, that she didn't want it to end. This moment was the moment she'd wanted all her life.

CHAPTER ELEVEN

It was Austin who finally broke away from their dance when it was plainly apparent that Molly wasn't going to. He didn't want to, but he was a little scared. Scared he was getting too close. Scared she was getting too attached. Scared her parents were going to turn a water hose on them at any moment.

And her mother was literally glaring at them through the window.

They sat back down, and Austin took a long gulp of ice water. He needed to cool down. It was November, so it wasn't hot outside, but he felt like a menopausal woman having a hot flash… or at least what he assumed that felt like.

"So, Blake…" Lydia said, drawing the name out as

if she was mocking him, "when did you dye your hair?"

Molly choked on the piece of bread she was eating and Austin reached under the table, squeezing her thigh. Dang she had nice thighs.

"Excuse me?"

"Well, in every picture Molly showed her friend Olivia, you had very blond hair. Of course, our daughter never showed us your picture, so I only have Olivia's word to go on."

"Mother, honestly! Would you like him to do a police lineup for you?"

"I'd like to make sure my daughter knows who she's dating."

"Lydia, enough." Finally, her father spoke up. Austin was wondering if he had a backbone somewhere in there.

"Pardon?" she said, turning to her husband with her lips sucked so tight it looked like she was drinking straight lemon juice from a straw. It was evident that George never challenged Lydia.

"Our daughter is twenty-two years old. She can make her own decisions, and I think we should just butt out."

The tension - and silence - was palpable. And awkward.

"I was going through an eighties phase, what can I say?" Austin finally said. "I used to do some modeling, so yes, I totally sent Molly my best modeling pictures with my highlighted hair. Imagine her surprise when I had brown hair. She was pretty irked at me, weren't you honey?" he said, looking lovingly at Molly and smiling.

"Yeah. I was so confused when I saw him, but he's even more handsome than I ever could've imagined," she said, and honest to God, it seemed like she was really talking about Austin. She didn't seem to be faking it at all. "I wouldn't want him to look like anyone else." She looked into his eyes for a moment longer than necessary and then turned back to her bread.

For someone so tiny, she sure could put away the carbs.

Under the table, she reached over and took his hand and squeezed it as if to say thank you, but then she pulled it away. He wanted to grab it again and never let it go, and that was the crux of the problem.

"THANK GOD THAT'S OVER," Molly said as she shut the door to her room. "What a nightmare."

"I couldn't believe it when your Dad spoke up. Go, Dad!" Austin said with a laugh as he peeled off his shirt and threw it over the back of the sofa.

Dear God in heaven. His chest was amazing, but even more amazing were the muscles stretched taut across his back.

"Um, what are you doing?"

"Taking off that hot shirt," he said as he unbuttoned his pants.

"Whoa! Now what are you doing?" she said, turning her head like she'd never seen a man undress before.

"Chill. I'm just taking off my jeans. I have boxer briefs on, see?" For some odd reason, she turned to see, but that didn't make things any better. In fact, it made them worse. He was standing there wearing black boxer briefs, tight against his very toned leg muscles, and she couldn't stop staring.

It was embarrassing. She started to wonder if she was paralyzed or something.

"Molly? You okay?" he said, waving his hand in front of her face.

She swallowed hard and managed to avert her eyes. "Yeah. Sorry. I was just thinking about something…"

"About what?" he asked, smiling like he knew

exactly what she was thinking. He walked toward her and closed the gap between them.

"About… finding my catfish, of course," she said, stepping back and taking off her earrings before putting them on the dresser. She could see Austin in her peripheral vision as he remained where he was and then finally turned to walk back toward his luggage. He took a pair of gray pajama pants from his bag and slipped them on.

"I've got some ideas on that. Just leave it to me."

She watched him in the dresser mirror, making sure he didn't see her. He looked so strong and confident, and she had no question that she could trust him to help her. It was a great feeling to know that someone had her back for once.

"Austin?" she said softly as she turned around. He was sitting on the sofa, his elbows rested on his knees.

"Yeah?"

"That dance tonight… Were you acting that way for my parents?" She sat down on the bed across from him.

"Acting what way?"

"Holding me so tightly… pulling me closer…"

Austin sighed, as if he was contemplating how to respond. His face softened in a way she hadn't seen, and he ran his fingers through his hair before finally looking back up at her.

"I wasn't acting, Molly."

Her breath caught in her throat. "Okay."

"What about you? Were you acting?" he asked quietly.

She looked down, wondering what to say. The answer to this question could turn her world upside down.

"No."

He stood up and walked toward her, pulling her hands until she was upright. His hand moved up and he brushed his thumb across her cheek, staring into her emerald green eyes.

"I don't know what to do about this," he said softly. "I've never been in this position before, Molly."

"What position?" she asked, her breath quickening.

"These feelings, I don't know what they are. I didn't mean for this to happen. I just wanted to help you, and I didn't really even know why…" He was almost pleading with her in some way, and she couldn't understand why. It was like he was fighting himself, like there was some battle inside of him that she couldn't see taking place, but she knew it was there.

He pulled her closer and buried his head into the nape of her neck and just held her there. She never wanted him to let go, and she had no idea what to say. Their backgrounds were so different, but in the end they both weren't accepted by their parents. They had that much in common.

He took a deep breath and finally broke away, but continued looking down at her with this tormented look in his eyes.

"What's wrong?" she asked.

"I am. I would be all wrong for you, and you've been hurt enough. I could kill that guy for stringing you along and making you think he loved you. I'm afraid of what I'll do when I find him," he said through gritted teeth.

"He's not worth it, Austin. I was just being gullible, like you said before…"

"No," he said, sliding his hand behind her head and looking into her eyes, "you were falling in love, but it was with the wrong man."

"And who is the right man, Austin?" she asked, barely able to continue standing. She wanted to melt into a puddle right then and there.

"I don't know…"

"I think you do."

"Molly, I can't..." he started to say, but there was a tap at the door.

"Molly? Do you have any extra shampoo? Your father apparently used all of mine," her mother - who had impeccable timing - asked through the door.

Austin rested his head against hers and sighed.

"Yes, Mom, I'll bring it right down in a second," Molly said. "I'm so sorry..."

"Go," he said. "It's okay."

"I'll be right back," she said, but she knew the conversation was probably over anyway. He had it in his head that he was all wrong for her, and she had no idea if he was right or not.

AUSTIN WATCHED her walk out the door, and he wanted to run. He literally wanted to pack up everything he'd brought with him to January Cove and bolt. This was too much - too many feelings, too much conflict welling up inside of him.

But he didn't leave people. No matter what. If there was one thing being abandoned by his own mother had taught him, it was that you never leave the people you love.

Wait, love? Oh no. Had he just said that? He didn't love her. No way. He barely knew her. Maybe he just thought she was hot. Surely that was it.

But he knew it wasn't.

MOLLY STOOD in her parent's room, listening to her mother drone on and on about Liam's newest accomplishment. He had called after dinner to tell them the details of his new promotion and how it would even take him to Hong Kong for a few months.

But all she could think about what Austin standing back in her room shirtless and possibly about to profess his undying love for her. She desperately wanted to get back into his arms and feel the beat of his heart against her cheek.

How had this all happened so fast? Was she being stupid and gullible again in her quest for finding a man to love her? That was her worst fear. How would she ever be able to trust her own instincts when it came to falling in love?

"Molly?" her mother said, standing there with her bathrobe on and her hands on her hips. "Are you even listening to me?"

"What? Oh, yeah. I was just thinking about some work stuff of my own," she said, jutting her chin out.

"About what? Coffee?"

"I've got to go, Mom," she said, heading toward the door.

"You know, Molly, you can do it too."

"Do what?" she asked, turning to face her mother.

"Make something of your life. You're still so young. You could come back to Seattle with us, go back to school, get a real degree," her mother was holding her hands now, smiling brightly and looking into her eyes. "We'll even pay for it, won't we George?"

Her father nodded and looked back down at his phone. Molly was livid and pulled her hands away.

"When are you going to actually listen to me?" she said loudly.

"Honey, I am listening to you, but you're not being reasonable!"

Molly walked to the door and opened it, ready to walk out.

"You know, Mom, I've tried my whole life to please you. I've tried to be the perfect daughter you always wanted, the female version of Liam. But I can't be something I'm not. I was awkward and shy and nerdy minus the smart part. I have dyslexia, and

I don't want to work in corporate America. I went all the way across the country to find the man of my dreams even when everyone thought I was nuts. I don't fit in, and I don't know why."

"Molly, that's just not true..."

"It is true, and you know it. I remember back in middle school, I was convinced I had to be adopted because I was so different from you and Dad and Liam. And I actually found myself hoping I was adopted because that would make more sense."

"You don't mean that."

"Yeah, I do. I love you guys, but the difference is that I accept you all for who you are, and you've never been able to do that for me. And honestly, I'm tired of trying."

"But, sweetie, don't you want more in your life?" she asked, a stray tear rolling down her cheek.

"More? What more do I need? I live in a beautiful town with nice people and no crime. I have some amazing new friends who really care about me and accept me for who I am. And I have a wonderful man who holds me up when I'm feeling down and thinks I'm perfect just the way I am. More money and a fancier car couldn't make me any happier. Why isn't it enough that your only daughter is actually happy? I'll tell you why. Because it reflects on you."

"I don't know what you mean…"

"You don't want to have to tell your fancy society friends that your only daughter lives in a little town in Georgia and works at a coffee shop. You want to tell them I either married rich or I'm a corporate lawyer or something, but God forbid I'm just a normal woman in love with a normal man living in a normal place. Terrible!" Molly said, pretending to gasp and putting her hand over her mouth before she walked out, shut the door and went back to her room.

When she opened the door to her room, she couldn't help the flow of emotion that sprang out of her. Tears flowed and she could hardly control her sobs as she slid down the door and onto the floor in an emotional mess. Austin was taking a shower, and the water shut off just as she started to catch her breath.

"Molly"! he said as he ran over to her, still wet from his shower and only wearing a towel. She was so upset that there was no time to even drool over his current attire. "What happened?"

She tried to catch her breath, but to no avail, so

she just sobbed more. Finally, after a few moments, she got it together enough to speak.

"My mom," she said, and then she started laughing. "That's about it."

Austin looked at her, makeup smeared, tears streaking down her face, and laughed with her. There they were - one sexy guy in a towel with wet hair and one tiny woman with a wet face - sitting in the floor laughing at absolutely nothing.

"I'm sorry. You must think I'm a raving lunatic," she said after a couple of minutes. He shook his head and wiped a stray tear away with his thumb.

"Nope. Just a regular human being." She smiled.

"My mother and I just had a little... discussion... and about twenty years of feelings came pouring out of me. I'm sure she was stunned to hear all that I said."

"And how do you feel now?"

"Lighter." And she did. She actually felt like a weight had been lifted from her shoulders. All those years she'd kept her feelings bottled up inside and tried to keep the peace, but now it was out there. All the ugliness was exposed to the light.

"Well, that's good then. Can I ask you a question?"

"Sure," she said.

"Do you like Friends?" he asked. It wasn't the question she expected him to ask in that moment.

"The TV show?"

"Yep."

"I love it! Why?"

"What do you say that we crawl up into your bed - totally platonic of course - and watch a marathon? I'll go make us some popcorn and we'll just lock ourselves away from the world tonight."

"That sounds perfect," she said. He leaned in and kissed her on the cheek.

"Then that's what we'll do. Let me get changed," he said as he stood up and walked to the bathroom. When the door shut, Molly sighed.

"And you're perfect too."

AUSTIN STARED at himself in the bathroom mirror. What was he doing? Instead of moving further away from her, he was moving closer. He was moving into her bed.

But she'd been crying. He couldn't tell her that they could only be friends, that he wasn't capable of trusting another woman with his heart. His mom had seen to that a long time ago.

Seeing her in a ball on the floor sobbing had ripped his heart out. He never wanted to see that again, and he certainly didn't want to be the one who caused her to do that.

Yet he knew it couldn't happen. He had to find her catfish and fast so that he'd have a reason to move on.

The only problem was, he didn't want to move on and that scared him to death.

CHAPTER TWELVE

Molly sat on her bed nervously waiting for Austin to return to the room. She could already smell the popcorn, so it wouldn't be long.

She had changed into her favorite pair of pajamas, a soft gray set with blousy pants and a long sleeved top. She turned on the gas logs in her fireplace, a perk of staying in an old antebellum B&B, and slid under the covers with only the light from the TV flickering in the room.

Platonic. He'd said it from the outset. Did he want it to be platonic? Did she? Was he just saying that to be a gentleman or because he was afraid she wanted more? Did she want more?

The questions were making her head spin.

"Hey, I hope you wanted some sweet tea. It's the only way I can eat popcorn," he said as he lightly kicked the door open and then closed it with his hip.

"Of course," she said, reaching across the bed and taking the tea. "Sweet and salty, the perfect combo."

He smiled. "We must have been separated at birth."

He put the bowl of popcorn between them and slid under the covers on his side of the bed, and Molly suddenly felt nervous because she had no idea where the night was going. There was a good two feet between them, but she could've sworn she felt the heat from his body radiating toward her. Maybe it was the warm popcorn in the bowl between them.

Austin reached for the remote and turned the channel to the marathon. "So, we're on the episode where Ross finds out Rachel has feelings for him," he said, taking a mouthful of popcorn.

"Do your male friends know you like this show?" she asked laughing.

"No, and we're not going to tell them," he said cutting his eyes at her. God, he was beautiful, especially when he smiled. That deep dimple made her feel weak every time she saw it.

"My lips are sealed," she said pretending to zip her lips.

They watched the show in silence, except for the sound of chewing popcorn and the occasional laugh. She'd seen these episodes a thousand times, but they never got old, and Austin seemed to be enjoying himself. When they both reached into the bowl at the same time and felt each other's hands instead of popcorn, she realized they'd reached the bottom.

He put the bowl on the nightstand and finished off his tea. And then he did something that shocked her. He patted the bed next to him and waved for her to come closer.

"I swear, I won't bite," he said softly. She wanted to ask if he might reconsider.

She scooted closer as he slid his arm around her, sending nerve impulses shooting through her body like never before. His hand came to rest on her shoulder, and she put her head down on his as they continued to watch the show. For a moment, she was convinced that he was smelling her hair again, but then he seemed to be looking at the TV.

All she knew was that this was the most confusing - but best - night of her life so far.

STOP SMELLING HER HAIR. Stop it! She's going to think you're some kind of weirdo, Austin thought to himself.

But he couldn't help it. What was that shampoo she was using? Strawberry, maybe? It smelled like heaven, even over the popcorn smell that was currently permeating the air in the room.

He was in bed with Molly. What was he doing? What kind of idiotic idea was this? Thank God he had a thick blanket over his waist or else she really might think he was a weirdo and that smelling her hair wasn't only one thing on his mind.

She was so perfect, right down to her little button nose and high pitched girly voice. She had a smattering of red freckles across her nose once her makeup was rubbed off a little, and her oversized pajamas were adorable on her.

Dear God, please divert my attention to this dang TV show. Help me continue to pretend I'm watching it and not daydreaming about her hair and nose, he thought.

He had been trying to do a good thing by comforting her, but now he'd gone over the line. He couldn't even see the line anymore. It was about ten miles back under a stack of burning tires.

How was he ever going to get out of this mess, especially when he had absolutely no desire to do so?

SHE COULD SMELL the faint scent of popcorn as she nuzzled her head deeper into the pillow. It was dark, except for the flickering light of the fire in the corner of the room. She pulled the cover up over her and sighed as she opened her eyes, and that's when she realized she wasn't lying on a pillow at all. It was Austin's chest.

He seemed to be asleep, only the faint rising and falling of his chest to let her know he was still alive. She could make out the silhouette of his strong jawline and those full lips of his as she popped her head up enough to see the clock on the nightstand. It was two thirty in the morning. The TV - thank goodness for sleep mode - had apparently turned itself at some point.

She surveyed her current situation. She was on her right side with her left leg slung over his knee. He was tilted toward her with both of his arms wrapped around her like she was a teddy bear. At some point, he had removed his shirt and her cheek was pressed against his bare skin.

Heaven. On. Earth.

She knew she shouldn't have done it, but she snuggled in closer, aching to just feel the warmth of him a while longer. Sooner or later, he'd wake up and realize they were entwined in each other's arms, but for now she had him all to herself.

Apparently, her little bit of movement alerted his body and he leaned in more, pulling her closer and pressing his lips to the top of her head. She froze in place, wondering what game she was playing. This wasn't how things were supposed to end up. He was her "pretend" boyfriend, only around to drive her parents crazy and keep them off her back. Things didn't seem so make-believe anymore.

As he leaned toward her and pulled her closer, she could feel something she hadn't expected. It was obvious he was either very attracted to her or having an amazing dream - or maybe both.

And then it happened. His hand reached down and tilted her chin upward toward his face, and his eyes looked straight into hers. He said nothing, just let out a breath and then what sounded like a growl and his mouth was on hers, pressing, searching hers.

She fell onto her back as he leaned over her, his elbows rested on the bed on either side of her head as he held her face.

"What are we doing?" she asked, barely able to get the words in between his urgent kisses.

"Pretending?" he asked with a hint of humor in his voice.

"But no one can see us…" she said as she ran her fingers up his back and drew him closer to her.

"Better to be safe than sorry," he said, kissing down her neck. "Good actors always practice, practice, practice."

"Oh, well don't let me stand in the way of good acting then," she said as she arched her head backward and gave him better access.

"Unless you want to stop?" he asked as he froze in place and looked down at her. "I don't want you to do anything you don't…"

She reached up and put her finger over his mouth. "You're interrupting a perfectly good scene, Austin. Take two!"

THE SUNLIGHT PEEKED through the wooden plantation shutters. Molly was on her left side now, Austin spooned around her like a blanket. He was still sleeping, at least judging from the heavy breathing she could hear.

She reached for her phone on the nightstand,

careful not to wake him up in the process. It was almost seven in the morning, and she needed to get to work. Thankfully, Rebecca was taking the early morning shift today so she still had an hour or so to get ready and grab breakfast.

"Hey," she whispered as she rubbed his arm, which was draped over her like he was in protection mode.

He made a grumbling noise, obviously not ready to wake up and leave their cocoon.

"Shhhh…" he said as he pressed his lips into the side of her neck and then up to her cheek. "Let's pretend we don't have jobs and aren't responsible members of society…"

"Austin…" she said, sounding like a purring kitten instead of a grown woman. He had a point. Being responsible and hard working was really a drag sometimes.

"Fine," he said as he pretended to let go but instead flipped her over onto her back and pressed his lips to hers. "Have we got just a few more minutes?"

She wanted to say no. She really did. But she couldn't. Her mouth had forgotten how to say those words to him.

MOLLY COULDN'T STOP SMILING no matter how hard she tried. Her cheeks were literally hurting, and she was sure that early wrinkles were on their way.

Even Rebecca had eyed her as she walked into work, asking what was going on with her. No way was she about to spill the beans on her beautiful, wonderful night with the most gorgeous man she'd ever seen.

Still, she worried. Where did this leave them? Were they dating? Was that just a one night stand? Did he just feel bad because she'd been crying?

So many questions and absolutely no answers.

And then, like a bucket of cold water, her mother appeared. Instead of hearing the happy little bell on the door of Jolt, it sounded like one of those scary gong noises you hear in the movies.

"Hello, Molly," her mother said. She was always so formal. Hello. How about "hi" or "howdy"?

"Good morning. What can I get you?" Molly said, trying her best to sound disinterested and not at all affected.

"Can we talk?"

"We talked last night." Molly continued wiping

down the counters around the cash register and hoped that another customer would walk in and break up their little chat, but that was unlikely. The lunch crowd, if you could call it that, wouldn't be in for at least another hour or so.

"I'm sorry you got so upset last night," her mother said. It wasn't really an apology for her behavior. It was an apology only that Molly got upset. Maybe her mother didn't think she was smart enough to pick up on that, but she was.

"Can we not do this again? This is my workplace, and even though this isn't important work as far as you're concerned, it is important to me. Please try to have even the tiniest amount of respect for that."

"I do respect your work, Molly. I just know that you're meant for greater things."

"Mom, this is my life, and I'm going to live it the way I want. Now, either you can deal with that and be happy that your only daughter is so content in her life, or you can just not be in my life at all." She couldn't believe she said it out loud, even though she'd thought it a million times before.

Her mother just stared at her with her mouth gaping open. "I can't believe you just said that."

"Well, I mean it. Respect goes both ways, and it's

about damn time I demanded it." She walked around the counter and started wiping tables.

"Molly James, don't you curse at me!"

Molly slowly turned around and walked toward her mother, leaving very little space between them.

"My whole life you've criticized me and pushed me around. No more. I'm not like you, any of you. I'm my own person, flaws and all. Either accept me for who I am, or get out of my life. It's very simple. The plane is going down, and I'm saving myself."

With that, Molly walked around the counter and started cleaning the espresso machine until she heard the door close behind her mother. She took a deep breath, wiped away a stray tear and continued cleaning.

AUSTIN SAT behind his desk in a daze. He was tired but wired, still high from being with Molly the night before. He thought he'd have regrets, and he'd feel a hell of a lot better if he did, but there were none. Every part of him was screaming that she was the one. THE one.

She was the elusive soulmate that he didn't even believe existed. Until today, soulmates were a myth that people made up to justify their choice in a mate. Now he knew he'd been wrong.

When he heard a knock at the door, he assumed that it was Molly coming by for a mid afternoon rendezvous, but it definitely wasn't Molly.

It was her mother.

"May I come in?" she asked. The woman was as stuffy as they came with her white wool coat and her straight skirt that fell just above her knee. He was surprised she didn't wear a fur muff and white gloves too.

"Of course. Come in. What can I do for you?"

"Stop seeing my daughter and convince her to come home."

"Wow. Way to cut to the chase, Mrs. James."

"I don't believe in mincing words." She sat down in front of him and held her purse close to her chest as if he was going to mug her or something.

"And why would I do that?"

"Because her life is in Seattle. She doesn't know what she's doing, and she needs some time to think about what she really wants in life."

"I think Molly can decide that for herself."

"She chased a complete stranger all the way here, and he didn't even exist!"

"I do exist," he said, trying to keep up the charade.

"You're not Blake, and I'm not an idiot. Your name is Austin York. I do my homework."

"What do you want from me?" he asked, leaning back in his chair.

"Let my daughter go, and I'll give you fifty-thousand dollars to start your own business. Start a brand new life."

"Excuse me?" He couldn't believe what he was hearing.

"I think it's a very reasonable offer. I've done some digging. I know you've had a rough past, and that's not what I want for my daughter. This is your chance."

"You mean it isn't what you want for your family. A kid who was abandoned by his drug addict mother, passed around from foster home to foster home. It's pretty seedy, huh?" he said, leaning over his desk as she clutched her purse tighter. "Well, let me tell you something. I can't be bought. I love your daughter, and that is worth a hell of a lot more than whatever you can offer me. Now get out."

She stood up slowly and walked toward the door, but not before turning around one more time.

"If you love her, then do the right thing for her. She has a bright future ahead of her... unless you take that away from her."

She walked out and shut the door behind her, and Austin was left reeling. Not from what she'd said as much as what he said. He loved her?

Damn it. He loved her.

CHAPTER THIRTEEN

Molly sat in her room wondering where he was. He was usually home by now, but it was getting dark and he still wasn't there. What was that about?

She decided to take a walk, clear her head. The altercation with her mother had really rattled her, and she needed to talk to someone but Austin wasn't there. He was just gone.

She walked past Jake's Bar and decided to go inside to get a glass of wine, and then she saw him. Austin was sitting at the bar nursing a beer and staring up at the TV. There was a football game on, but he seemed to be looking right through the screen.

"Hey," she said softly, touching his shoulder. He

jumped, almost as if she'd burned him with her hand.

"Hey." He didn't even turn around, just kept drinking. He smelled like he'd been drinking for a while, and when she sat down she could see that his eyes were bloodshot.

"You didn't come home."

"First of all, that isn't home. It's a freaking bed and breakfast. And it's a room. And it's not even my room." He was definitely slurring his words.

"Okay..."

"And second of all... Damn it, I forgot the second thing."

"Austin, let's get you... back to the room..." She pulled on his arm, but he jerked away.

"You're not my wife! You're not even my girl-friend! So back off."

Tears welled in her eyes. How could she have been so wrong about him? Why was he hurting her after comforting her last night?

Apparently he wanted one thing, and when he got it... it was over. She felt like a fool.

"Austin, I don't understand..."

He turned and looked at her, quickly averting his eyes away from her face. "Molly, I tried to tell you that this isn't going to work. You need to move on."

She stood there, embarrassed and confused, as he slapped the bar and attempted to order another beer. The bartender shook his head.

"Dude, you've had enough. Why don't you let your girlfriend take you home?"

"I'm not his girlfriend," Molly said softly and then walked out.

AUSTIN WOKE up in his own bed across the hall from Molly. It was one in the morning and he felt sick. He couldn't remember everything that had happened, but he knew it wasn't good. The only way to make her hate him was to make him hate himself at the same time.

His eyes felt like they were covered in sandpaper, and his tongue had some kind of coating. He wasn't a big drinker normally, so this wasn't a good feeling at all. He felt sick and nauseous and hungry at the same time, but he wasn't about to eat anything for fear of running into Molly.

Was she crying right now? Was she completely hurt and confused? He hated the thought of her sweet face crying again, and this time because of him.

But it was the only answer. He needed to get his hands on that fifty-thousand dollars, and this was the only way to make it happen.

He'd made a deal with the devil, and there was no going back now.

"Good morning, Molly," Addison said in her normal chipper tone the next morning. Molly had taken the day off work, unable to get any sleep the night before. She had tossed and turned and alternated between crying fits and punching her pillow.

"Good morning," she muttered as she reached for the coffee pot and realized it was empty. And then she burst into tears.

"Oh, sweetie, what's wrong?" Addison asked, pulling her into a hug.

"What isn't wrong? It's all wrong…"

"Does this have anything to do with Austin moving out this morning?"

She froze in place, her lungs devoid of air. "He left?"

"Yeah. Said he had some business in Atlanta and would be gone for a few days or maybe even weeks."

"So he's gone?" She couldn't believe it. That was

it. There was no fixing it. He just abandoned her and the beginning of their beautiful relationship without a thought. He took what he wanted from her and he left.

Molly sat down on the bar stool and stared into the garden through the bay window. They'd sat on those benches eating banana pudding.

"Can you tell me what happened?" Addison asked again.

Molly told her everything. The whole story. Even the part she was most embarrassed about.

"I don't know how I could've been so wrong about him. About us."

"I don't understand either. He seems like such a nice guy," Addison said, and she truly did look confused. "I really thought you were perfect for each other."

Before they could continue their conversation, Molly's mother appeared in the doorway.

"I'm going to go check on Anna Grace. She's napping in the front room," Addison said as she excused herself.

"Have you been crying? What's wrong?" her mother asked, sounding genuinely concerned.

"Nothing."

"Is this about Austin?" her mother asked. How

did she know his name?

"You mean Blake?"

"Honey, I know. I've known for a while."

"Wait. How did you…"

"It's not important. Let's just say I was protecting my daughter as best I could… even if she didn't want me to." Lydia sat down next to Molly and rubbed her leg.

"I guess you were right. He wasn't the man for me." She hated to admit it, but what other conclusion was there? She stared off in the distance, completely exhausted with the events of the last twenty-four hours.

"Molly, why don't you come home with us? Stay for a few weeks. Get your bearings. See Olivia. Let us try to start over."

"I love my life here. Or at least I did…" She was so confused, so tired.

"You don't have to stay in Seattle. Just take a couple of weeks. Come home for Thanksgiving."

She couldn't believe she was considering it, but familiarity sounded safe right now. Twenty-four hours ago, Austin was her only safe place.

"Okay," she said as her mother hugged her. It felt so hollow, but she accepted it anyway.

THE FLIGHT HAD BEEN LONG, but thankfully she slept most of the time. Her dreams were about Austin, and her nightmares were about him too. She was standing at the edge of a ravine, and he just walked by and pushed her over the edge. Very fitting.

The next few days were spent seeing Olivia, spending time with her mother and resting as much as she could. But nothing was taking the pain away. Blake was just a blip in her memory when compared with Austin. He was the one for her, she'd been so sure of it.

Maybe she should stop trusting her gut because it was obviously not working.

She went out to the mailbox after being back in Washington for six days and found a letter addressed to her. She opened it and found a plain white piece of paper with unfamiliar handwriting. But then she saw the signature. Austin.

It was a simple note that said:

I found your catfish and they're right in your back-yard. Blake was never a guy. It was a girl, and her name is Megan Towns. I hope you're well.

— Austin

The content of the note didn't register with her

at first. Seeing his name, touching his handwriting - those were the things that wounded her soul. And then she smelled the paper, the familiar fragrance of his cologne lingering on it. She wanted to put it on her pillow and sleep with her cheek against it tonight in the hopes of reliving the memories of their one night together.

As she drifted back to her senses a few minutes later, it hit her. Megan Towns. That name was familiar. She pulled her high school yearbook from under her bed and found the name.

Megan had been another "reject" at their high school. She was masculine and definitely an outcast. They hadn't been friends or enemies, really. In fact, she couldn't remember ever talking to Megan face to face.

Why would she do this?

All of the pent-up frustration of the last year came bubbling up to the surface and suddenly anger appeared. Why would this girl do such a hurtful thing to her, a perfect stranger?

She had gone all the way across the country looking for someone who didn't even exist, and now she was heartbroken for a second time over a man who did exist but didn't want her.

And there was only one thing to do. She was

going to confront Megan Towns before the sun went down.

FOR THE SECOND time in the last few weeks, she stood in front of a door. This time, she didn't expect to see the love of her life; she expected to see a liar.

She didn't wait around, but instead pounded on the door and shouted.

"Megan Towns! Come out here right now!" Surely the neighbors in her apartment complex would call the police any second, but Molly didn't care. She wanted answers and she wanted them now. She banged on the door again and again until she heard someone walking toward it and turning the handle.

And there she was. Megan Towns. She looked nothing like she had in high school now. Instead, she was a good fifty pounds heavier with jet black hair, a mohawk and what appeared to be a dog collar for a necklace.

But the look on her face when she saw Molly was one of pure shock, and maybe a little fear. Here stood Molly, five foot nothing, with her petite little frame and squeaky voice. She was no physical match for Megan, but she could more than make up for it in anger.

She wanted to scream and yell, but stopped herself when she saw the look on Megan's face. It was soft and stunned, and her eyes were welling with tears.

"Molly James?" she whispered.

"You know exactly who I am, Megan." Megan nodded her head and stared down at her feet.

"I'm so sorry. It got out of hand." And there it was. An admission of guilt and immediate repentance. All of the hopes and dreams of "Blake" vanished in the blink of an eye. It was almost like her life was flashing before her as her brain scanned through every text message with "him". It was all passing away, drifting into the energetic space of things that never really happened.

"Why did you do this to me? What did I ever do to you?" Molly asked.

"Would you like to come inside?" Megan asked, holding the door open. The place was dark and dingy, and Molly definitely didn't feel safe going in alone.

"No, thank you. I just need an answer. I think you owe me that much. This has turned my entire life upside down."

"Let's sit," Megan said, pointing to a concrete table and bench set in the garden area next to her apartment. Molly nodded and sat down as Megan sat across from her. She was nervous, that much was plainly obvious from the way she was fidgeting with her hands and looking down.

Molly waited a few moments, hoping the answer would come, but Megan said nothing. She just kept taking deep breaths like she was trying to ward off a panic attack.

"Are you going to explain?"

Megan finally looked up. "I'm so sorry. I never meant to screw your life up. It just went too far."

"Why did you do this?"

"I had a crush on you in high school."

Molly was stunned. She barely remembered this person, so the thought that someone - especially another girl - had a crush on her back then wasn't even a thought in her mind until now.

"Um... I don't... I'm not..."

"I know you're not a lesbian, Molly," Megan said with a sad smile. "That's why I never said anything. But when I saw you on Facebook, I was desperate to talk to you. Look, my high school experience wasn't good."

"And neither was mine," Molly said, "but that

didn't give you the right to lie to me and make promises you couldn't keep. You dragged me along for a year, Megan. A year!"

"I know, and I'm so so sorry. I just didn't know how to stop."

"And why January Cove of all places?"

"I took a trip there at the end of last summer with my cousin, Hillary. We were there for a week, and that's when I gave you that address. I regretted it later, but I hoped you'd lose it or forget about it."

"And the man's voice on our phone calls?"

"Me."

Molly's stomach churned. All this time, she'd held out hope that her catfish was at least a man, maybe someone who wanted to talk to her but was too scared. But this wasn't something she'd even considered.

"You know, all this time I thought someone hated me enough to string me along, probably laughing at me the whole time."

"No, I don't hate you, Molly!" Megan said, attempting to reach out and touch her hand. Molly pulled her hand back.

"I have to go…"

"Can you forgive me?" Megan asked, standing up with tears running down her face.

"Look, I know what it's like to not be accepted, to not be loved. But I also know what it's like to finally find that person who accepts you for who you are and how great that feels, even if just for a short time. It's worth going for, Megan. It's worth fighting for. I truly hope you find happiness in your life, and I already forgive you. I know you did this from a place of pain."

Megan looked so relieved. Molly was telling the truth. She felt nothing for "Blake" anymore. She didn't feel upset about the trek across the country or any of it. It was like some distant past memory that didn't matter anymore. She'd somehow let it go.

Because of Austin. At least she was thankful for that.

"Thank you," Megan said softly.

"Good luck to you," Molly said, walking over and shaking her hand. "I hope you find what you're looking for."

With that, she left her anger and bitterness behind, and she got in her car to drive home.

WHEN MOLLY GOT BACK HOME, her mother was sitting at the kitchen table looking over some paperwork.

"Oh, hi, honey. Where were you?"

"Confronting my catfish."

"Huh?"

"My catfish. The person who pretended to be Blake."

"You found him?"

"Her."

"What?" Her mother dropped her paperwork and looked at her with her mouth hanging open.

"Yep. Actually Austin found her and sent me a note."

"And how did she respond?"

"She was very apologetic and sad. I forgave her."

"That's amazing, Molly. I don't know if I would have been so quick to forgive." Her mother sounded genuinely impressed.

"I surprised myself," she said with a laugh. "I guess I needed to forgive for my own sanity, and it's hard to be angry about it when I got so much good from it."

"Good?" she asked as Molly sat down at the table.

"Yeah. I was thinking about it as I drove over here. Knowing that Blake loved me this year gave me confidence and peace for the first time since I was a little kid. And then meeting everyone in January

Cove. Well, that was the best gift of all. Those people were kind and accepting of me, and I felt good about myself and the person I was becoming there. And Austin... It didn't end well, and I still don't know why, but he made me feel things I've never felt before."

Her mother looked at her, a sad expression on her face. But Molly didn't have time to question her before the doorbell rang. It was a man wearing a suit and holding a big envelope.

"Molly James?" he said.

"Yes..."

"I have a delivery for you. Can we talk for a minute... alone?" he asked, looking past her into the kitchen. She nodded and walked out onto the landing.

"What's going on?"

"I can't go into a lot of details, but this paperwork is a trust that was set up in your name... anonymously. It's for fifty-thousand dollars. The person who set it up doesn't want to be named or thanked, but wanted me to deliver a message to you."

She couldn't breathe or speak so she just nodded. He began to read.

"*This money is about freedom. It's here for you to use however you wish so that you can create the life of your dreams. Money gives you choices, and this is your chance to choose exactly what you want, on your own terms."*

"I don't understand… Who…" she stammered as she took the envelope. He nodded for her to open it. She wasn't a lawyer, but all of the papers looked completely legal and legit to her.

"Good luck, Miss James."

The man walked down the stairs and to his black BMW as she stood there shocked. After he drove away, she turned back to the house.

"Honey, are you okay? Who was that man?" her mother asked as she rushed to her side. Molly sat on the bottom of the steps in the foyer.

"You're not going to believe this. Some anonymous person set up a trust fund for me… with fifty-thousand dollars!" she said, grinning from ear to ear as tears ran down her face. But her mother didn't look excited. She looked shocked. Scared. Pale. "Mom, what's wrong?"

"Oh, God, I think I've made a terrible mistake. I think I was completely wrong about something…"

"What?"

"You're going to hate me…"

"What did you do, Mom?" Molly asked, knowing full well this wasn't going to be good.

CHAPTER FOURTEEN

I t had been two weeks since Molly left Seattle to make her permanent home in January Cove. Whether she ever saw Austin again, she knew this place was her home.

She was being very careful with her trust fund money, putting most of it in savings but paying the rent on her new little cottage style house for a whole year up front. It was nice to have her own space, although she visited Addison often and had even babysat for Anna Grace a couple of times.

Leaving Seattle hadn't been hard at all, but forgiving her mother for what she'd done had been almost impossible. In the end, she did forgive her after her mother apologized and realized her huge mistake. She'd stolen the love of Molly's life away from her.

Even though she knew Austin had set up the trust fund, she still couldn't reach him to at least say thank you. She called his old number, but it was disconnected. She called Ballard, but they claimed to not know where he was and they'd put some other guy in charge of the January Cove property.

He seemed to have vanished into thin air. She hoped he was okay, but she had decided to move forward in her life. After all, her life had been in limbo for over a year before she even came to January Cove in the first place.

Megan had actually texted her one more time, telling her she was sorry. Molly accepted the apology again and then changed her phone number. That chapter was done.

She had a fresh start, although seeing places that she went to with Austin still bothered her. She loved him, although she'd never said it before. She missed him.

Today was Thanksgiving, and it was a time to be grateful for the people who were in her life. The Parker family had invited her to a big gathering at the B&B, and she was excited to go and meet the rest of the family.

She'd made a big salad for the event, so she left a bit early to walk over. Thankfully, it was only two blocks from her new home.

"Molly! Come in!" Addison said, giving her a quick hug. "I'm so glad you could join us today."

"Thank you for inviting me. Otherwise, I'd be alone," Molly said. "And eating a frozen turkey dinner in your yoga pants is not a great Thanksgiving." Addison giggled.

"Yeah, I wouldn't think so. Here, let me take that." She took the salad and carried it into the kitchen. "Everyone should start arriving in about half an hour."

"Is there anything I can help you with?"

"Actually, yes. I left my good tablecloth in the hope chest in your old room. Would you mind digging it out for me?"

It was a strange request, but she nodded her head and went up the stairs. One of the last times she'd been in that room, Austin had held her close. She wasn't sure she even wanted to open the door, but she couldn't tell Addison no.

She opened the door and went straight to the hope chest, trying not to even look at the bed. But she couldn't help herself. She stood there, staring at it, allowing one stray tear to fall from her cheek.

A hand touched her shoulder, and she jumped, dropping the tablecloth in the floor. She turned, ready to punch somebody's lights out, and found Austin standing there. He'd been hiding in the closet.

"I'm sorry. I didn't mean to scare you..."

"Really? By hiding and then touching me from behind?" she said, still trying to catch her breath and holding her chest. Then the realization that Austin was standing there in front of her, in the flesh. She couldn't reach out and hug him. The last time he'd seen her, he had been so mean and vicious. "How are you?"

"Awful."

"Really? Why?" she asked, crossing her arms.

"Because being without you is hell on Earth."

Her heart skipped a beat. "But, you said..."

"Molly, you're a smart girl. Don't you understand that I had to be the world's biggest jackass to make our breakup believable so your mom would give me that money?"

"I could've asked my parents for money, Austin!"

"Not without strings, you couldn't."

He was right about that much. "Then why didn't you tell me what she was doing?"

"Because you're too good a person to defraud your own mother. Look, I had to get that money for you, and I had to show your mother that I love you all at the same time."

She couldn't breathe. He loved her. He loved her. She just kept hearing a voice say it in her head over and over.

"You… love me?"

He walked closer and ran his hands up her arms. "Of course I do. I think you know that," he said softly.

"I… wasn't sure…"

"I gave you fifty-thousand dollars, Molly."

"And then you disappeared."

"I needed time."

"For what?"

"To make peace with my own past. To figure out if I'm truly good enough for you."

"And you did that?" she asked, looking up at him.

"Not really. I don't think I'll ever be good enough for you, but I trust your judgment. I can't keep running from my own past. The only thing I can do is focus on a future, and I want that future to be with you. That is absolutely the only thing I'm sure of in my life."

She had never heard more beautiful words. "So you're staying in January Cove?"

"I'm staying wherever you're staying, Molly James."

There was that cute dimple again, the one she wanted to lick right about now.

"I love you," she said with a big grin as she threw her arms around his neck.

"I love you too."

"And if you ever act like that to me again, pretend or not, I'll hurt you!" she said as she smacked him on the back.

"Noted."

THE PARKER FAMILY gathered around the large table in the dining room, Clay sitting at the head of the table about to carve the turkey. It was the perfect picture of family and fun.

"I'd like to propose a toast," Addison said as she stood beside Clay. "To my brothers and their beautiful ladies, may God continue to bless you with years of special moments ahead. I'm so thankful for you and the closeness we all share."

"Hear, hear!" Brad yelled as his girlfriend, Ronni, lightly slapped him on the arm.

"Mind if I make a toast?" Austin asked, which was

completely out of character for him. Addison smiled and nodded. He stood up, glass of sweet tea in hand and raised it up. "Over the course of my life, I haven't had a lot to be grateful for, or at least that's what I thought. A few weeks ago, that all changed when one beautiful woman smiled at me for the first time. Well, actually, she knocked me over the first time she met me. And then she was rude for awhile…"

"Dude, I think you're messing this toast thing up…" Clay said under his breath. Everyone laughed.

"Anyway, today I just want to say how thankful I am for Molly because she has shown me what love really is and I can't wait to share the rest of my Thanksgivings with her."

A collective "awwww" filled the room as Molly grinned from ear to ear. She wanted to say her own toast, but everyone was ready to eat and Anna Grace was already wiggling in her highchair. When the room was loud again, she leaned over to Austin and said, "Today, I'm thankful for Fake Blake."

He smiled and nodded in agreement.

READY TO READ MORE of this series? Be sure to check out my store where you can get special deals by clicking HERE.

You can also find my books on Amazon by clicking HERE

Want to find out about all of my new releases! You can get on my VIP reader list by clicking HERE.

Made in the USA
Coppell, TX
20 June 2023

18308828R00125